Program for Destruction

As soon as Frank and Joe stepped inside the building, they heard screams of panic. Then a huge crowd of people came running down the hall right at them. But if the assembly line was still working, why had the people run away?

They found the answer when they entered the main floor of the factory. The computer-controlled assembly line robots had gone totally berserk!

One robot was throwing fenders in every direction. Another was ripping the doors off car bodies, while yet another one crashed down on the middle of the assembly line, smashing windshields and denting hoods, roofs, and trunks.

It was the same everywhere they looked. The robots were turning the factory into a car junkyard!

The Hardy Boys Mystery Stories

Available from MINSTREL Books

87

The HARDY BOYS®

PROGRAM FOR DESTRUCTION

FRANKLIN W. DIXON

A MINSTREL® BOOK

PUBLISHED BY POCKET BOOKS

New York   London   Toronto   Sydney   Tokyo

A MINSTREL PAPERBACK *ORIGINAL*

 A Minstrel Book published by
POCKET BOOKS, a division of Simon & Schuster Inc.
1230 Avenue of the Americas, New York, N.Y. 10020

ISBN: 0-671-64895-0

Produced by Mega-Books of New York, Inc.

First Minstrel Books printing November, 1987

10 9 8 7 6 5 4 3

Contents

PROGRAM FOR DESTRUCTION

1 Car of the Future

"What do you think is wrong with it?" Frank Hardy asked, sticking his head under the hood of the dark blue van.

"Don't know," replied his brother, Joe, with a shrug of his muscular shoulders. He ran his fingers through his blond hair. "When I tried getting it started the engine kicked over once. Then it died. I promised Mom I'd mail some information to Dad up in Boston for that case he's working on, and—" He stopped and said, "What's the matter?"

Frank was staring at his brother. "You were going to drive to the post office?"

"I know what you're thinking," Joe said with a grin. "You're thinking the post office is just a few blocks away."

"You're a mind reader."

"And you're thinking that your little brother is getting to be too lazy to walk if he can drive."

1

"This is amazingly on target." Frank laughed. "Keep going."

Joe obliged, saying, "You're also thinking that because the van wouldn't start, I didn't mail that stuff to Dad. Am I right?"

"Absolutely, totally right."

"Frank, Joe!" called Laura Hardy from the front door of their house.

Frank and Joe turned and saw their mother rushing down the front walk. "I'm off to the beauty parlor," Mrs. Hardy announced. "See you later," she said as she passed them on the driveway, giving each of them a kiss on the cheek.

"And thanks, Joe," she added, "for mailing that envelope and picking up the dry cleaning this morning. I know you had a long walk with the van not working, and I appreciate it. Well, so long."

As their mother hurried off to have her hair done, Joe smiled triumphantly at his brother, and his blue eyes sparkled. "Now you're thinking that you ought to say you're sorry."

"Best mind reader in Bayport." Frank grinned. "I apologize. I should know better than to sell you short," he said.

"Now that that's settled, what do you say we figure out what's wrong with our van?"

2

suggested Joe. "I mean, we're supposed to be super detectives, right?"

Frank nodded, and the two of them started testing every wire and connection under the van's hood. The van was a used police vehicle that had been given to the Hardys by Chief Ezra Collig of the Bayport Police. Frank and Joe depended on it for just about every case that came their way.

Checking the van was hot, dirty work, but they kept at it. Both of them were good with cars, but they still couldn't find the problem. They tested the sparkplugs, battery, and electrical system. Everything seemed to be in perfect working order.

Frank and Joe ignored the hot, muggy afternoon air and the cloudy sky that threatened rain. They also ignored the oil fumes rising from the engine and their growing frustration. They needed to get their van working again. Without wheels they were totally stranded.

"Hey!" a harsh voice called out, breaking into their concentration.

Frank and Joe pulled their heads out from underneath the hood and looked toward the street. They saw a well-dressed man sitting at the wheel of a sleek, shiny black sports car. The two-door car had a long, sloping

3

hood and rear. A gold racing stripe slashed across the side from front to back.

Frank shifted his gaze from the gleaming sports car to the man behind the wheel.

"Are you talking to us?" Frank asked politely.

The man ignored Frank's question and demanded, "Is this Fenton Hardy's house?"

Frank nodded.

"Good." The driver—a tall, heavyset man —got out of his car and immediately headed up the front walk.

"Uh . . . excuse me, sir," Frank called out.

The man pretended not to hear him and continued toward the door of the house.

Frank was going to tell him that nobody was home, but Joe touched his brother's arm and shook his head. "If he doesn't want to talk to you, that's his problem," Joe said softly.

"Right," Frank agreed.

He and Joe watched as the man rang the bell and stood there impatiently, drumming his fingers against his thigh. He rang it again, then a third time. Finally, he turned and marched back down the front walk. When he reached Frank and Joe, he demanded, "Where's Fenton Hardy?"

"I tried to tell you," said Frank. "He's not here. Our dad's out of town on a case."

"When will he be back?" asked the man quickly, a note of desperation creeping into his voice.

"We don't know," offered Joe. "It could be several days."

The news about Fenton Hardy seemed to make the tall, broad-shouldered man visibly wilt. He lowered his head and let out a deep sigh.

"Can we give him a message for you?" asked Frank, suddenly feeling sorry for the stranger.

"No, I can't wait for him to come back," he replied. "I need help right away." With that, he hurried on toward his car. But when he reached the driver's door he suddenly spun around. "Hey," he demanded, "did I hear you right? Did you say that Fenton Hardy is your father?"

"That's correct," Frank said quietly.

The stranger chuckled. "I thought you were a couple of kid mechanics. But you're those young detectives I've heard so much about, aren't you?"

"I don't know what you've heard," Frank said modestly, "but, yes, we've been known to crack a few cases."

5

The man walked toward them. "Well," he said, "I don't know where else to turn. Maybe you two can help me out until your father gets back."

The stranger stuck out his hand and said, "I guess I ought to introduce myself. My name is Arnold Stockard, president of the CompuCar Company."

Frank and Joe held up their oil-smeared hands, and Stockard grinned. "I've been known to get my hands dirty, myself, but thanks for the warning."

The boys introduced themselves by name and then Joe asked, "What's your problem, Mr. Stockard?"

"Sabotage," he replied darkly. "And if it isn't stopped soon, it'll put me out of business. I've got the most advanced sedans and sports cars on the market," he continued. "That's one of my sports cars," he said, proudly pointing at his shiny black car. "It's a CC-2000, and there's nothing like it in the world. There's an on-board computer built into these babies that makes them the ultimate in driving machines."

"I've been reading about them in some of my car magazines," commented Frank. "They're pretty amazing."

"It's only the beginning," Stockard boasted. "Someday everybody will drive a

6

CompuCar. It's the automobile of the future. My problem, though," he went on, "is that my company might never make it to the future. There's been a string of suspicious accidents and equipment failures at my factory. Somebody is trying to put me out of business. I want you to find who it is—and I want him stopped!"

"Have you contacted the police yet?" Joe wanted to know.

Stockard shook his head. "I want to keep this thing quiet," he said. "If I tell the police, the newspapers will get word of the situation and I don't need the bad publicity: It would ruin my reputation."

He added, "My employees have all been told not to say anything to anyone outside of work—not even their families!"

Frank and Joe looked at each other. It sounded like an interesting case. But there was just one little problem.

"We'd like to help you," admitted Frank, "but I don't think we can take on any cases right now."

"Why not? What's the problem?"

"It's really pretty simple," explained Frank. "Our van isn't running, and we're kind of stuck."

"We can't do any serious sleuthing by foot," added Joe.

7

"Don't worry about that," Stockard said, with a smile. "You forget, I'm in the transportation business. I'll make you a deal. If you go right to work on this sabotage case, I'll let you use one of my CC-2000's until you get your van running again. What do you say?"

Frank and Joe looked at the gleaming, ultramodern sports car parked in front of their house. Driving a machine like that sounded great. The two brothers looked at each other and nodded.

"You've got yourself a deal, Mr. Stockard," said Frank.

After Frank and Joe washed the grease off their hands and left a note for their mother, they joined Arnold Stockard in his CC-2000.

"I'll take you right over to the showroom and get you a car of your own," Stockard promised. Then he pushed a button on the steering wheel and said, "Let's go." Instantly, the car did exactly as Stockard ordered, pulling away from the curb and practically sailing down the street.

It was the smoothest ride Frank and Joe had ever experienced. But even more impressive than that, the dashboard of the car looked like the cockpit of a jet airplane.

There were gauges and dials with flashing lights and digital numbers wherever they looked.

"As you may have noticed," Stockard said, giving them a rundown of the car's features, "my voice pattern has been programmed into the on-board computer. The car will respond to my commands only. When I tell it to start or stop, it does just that. From a security angle, the voice activation system makes a CompuCar virtually impossible to steal.

"Whenever I want to talk to the car," he explained, "I push this button on the steering wheel." He hit the button and said, "How long will it take to reach the showroom if I stay on the main roads and travel within the posted speed limits?"

An electronic voice replied, "We'll reach your requested destination in eleven minutes and seventeen seconds."

"How much fuel will I have left when I arrive?"

"Sixteen point three one gallons," answered the car's computer voice.

Stockard glanced at Frank and Joe. "Impressed?"

"We're going to have to talk to our van about this," said Joe with a straight face.

Just then the car phone rang. "Yes?"

Stockard said into the receiver. "Of course I remembered the meeting. But I'm glad you called, Claypool. Please prepare a CC-2000 for Frank and Joe Hardy. It's for their personal use while they, uh, do a little personal investigating for me over at the factory. . . . Right, you know what I'm referring to. . . . Yes, I'm bringing them over to the showroom myself. We'll be there in just a little while.

"By the way," he continued, "how is the construction going on the roof over there? . . . I see. . . . Well, tell them to stop taking so many breaks and maybe they'd finish."

Stockard angrily hung up and said to the Hardys, "They're building a health club on the roof of the building where my showroom is located, and they never seem to finish. All that construction noise is bad for business, but every time you turn around the work crew is on a break.

"Oh well," he added with a sigh. "That isn't your problem. The important thing is that Gil Claypool, my showroom manager, will see to it that you get your car."

A few minutes later they pulled up in front of the CompuCar showroom. But Stockard didn't get out. "I'm going to have to head directly for a meeting," he apologized. "I'll see you at the factory later and show you around. I'm hoping that maybe you'll be able to pick up some clues."

"It's the logical place to start," agreed Frank.

They shook hands with Stockard and said they'd see him later. Then Frank and Joe got out of the car, closed the passenger door, and watched Arnold Stockard drive away.

"That sure was some car," said Joe.

"Tell me something I don't know," Frank said with a grin as they strolled across the sidewalk toward the showroom.

Just then a drop of water hit Joe on the nose. "Looks like it's finally going to rain," he said, as he absently glanced up at the dark sky.

But when he looked up, his eyes grew wide with horror. A huge steel beam was hurtling down from the roof of the building.

And it was falling straight toward them!

2 A Warning

There was no time to alert Frank. Instead, Joe leapt at his brother.

"Hey!" Frank shouted, shocked by the sudden attack. Joe, shorter and broader than his brother, managed to knock Frank down, and the two of them toppled over and rolled into the street.

An instant later there was a terrible boom, followed immediately by a crunching sound as the steel beam crashed against the sidewalk, shattering the concrete. Joe glanced at the beam, lying a few feet away from them. It was bent and twisted. He knew that if he had been a split second slower, this case would have been closed in a hurry!

"Are you all right?" Joe asked his brother. Frank had had the wind knocked out of him, but he managed to look over his shoulder at the broken sidewalk and gasp, "Yeah . . . I'm all right . . . thanks to you."

The blare of a car's horn made them realize that they were still lying in the street. Joe helped his brother up and they scrambled out of the road, back onto the sidewalk in front of the CompuCar showroom. A crowd of passersby quickly formed around them, telling them how lucky they were that they hadn't been killed.

Frank and Joe both happily agreed.

A dour-looking man with a shaggy head of curly brown hair looked up at the roof and said, "That sure was a curious kind of accident."

"What do you mean?" asked Frank, staring at the man.

"Look up there yourself and see," the man replied. "There aren't any workers on the roof."

Frank nudged his brother and the two of them looked up. Despite the light drizzle that was falling, they could see that the man was right. The roof looked deserted.

"I guess the beam must have been badly balanced when the workers left and it fell off the roof by itself," reasoned Joe.

"Possible," said the man, but he didn't sound as if he believed it.

"You've got something on your mind. What is it?" asked Frank, his brown eyes studying the man's face.

"Me? I don't have anything on my mind except looking for a job. Arnold Stockard had me fired today, and I don't mind saying that I wish that miserable excuse for a human being was lying underneath that steel beam right now."

The man began to walk away.

"What's your name?" asked Frank, following after the former CompuCar employee.

"Dennis . . . Dennis Belfree."

"We've heard that there have been a lot of accidents at CompuCar lately, Mr. Belfree," Frank said. "Maybe this was another one. But maybe it wasn't an accident." Frank looked the man straight in the eye. "Do you have any idea who would want to do something like this?" he asked innocently.

Belfree laughed. "If you think I'm the only guy who has it in for Stockard, then you don't know the CompuCar Company. Everybody there hates Arnold Stockard."

Joe signaled to his brother that he was going into the CompuCar showroom. Frank nodded. He knew that Joe probably wanted to talk to Gil Claypool, the manager, about the accident. Meanwhile, Frank planned to find out why everybody hated Arnold Stockard.

14

Walking a little farther away from the crowd, Frank asked, "What's so bad about Arnold Stockard?"

"You really want to know?"

"I wouldn't have asked if I didn't mean it," he replied, hoping to get the unhappy former employee to open up.

Dennis Belfree didn't need much prodding. He was so angry over being fired that once he started talking, it was hard for him to stop.

"Stockard isn't the man he pretends to be, and that's the truth," Belfree began. "He practically stole the CompuCar Company from its original founders, Robert Blane and Alan Krisp. He cheated them out of their fair share of the company. Of course you never hear about that. You never hear about a lot of stuff."

Belfree's face turned red with anger. "Stockard's supposed to be a genius, the next Henry Ford, but he only cares about making money; he doesn't care about the people who work for him. He shouts and screams and gives impossible orders. And then when you don't do what he wants, he fires you on the spot."

"Why did he fire you?" asked Frank.

"I was a showroom salesman," explained

15

Belfree. "When I went for a long stretch without selling a CompuCar, he told me to get out."

"If he's that lousy a boss," suggested Frank, "maybe you're better off not working for Stockard. There are other jobs, other employers."

Belfree scratched the side of his head in silence, thinking about what Frank Hardy had said. "You know," he finally replied, "you're probably right. Arnold Stockard and I just never got along. Anyway, sorry to lay all that on you. I guess I just needed to get it off my chest. Know what I mean?"

"Sure," said Frank. "No problem. I was glad to listen. And Mr. Belfree?"

"Yeah?"

"Good luck finding a new job."

When Frank caught up to his brother in the showroom, Gil Claypool came forward and announced, "I'm awfully sorry about that accident outside. You sure you're all right?"

"Just fine," said Frank. "Met an interesting guy out there, though. Maybe you know him. Dennis Belfree?"

The showroom manager rolled his eyes. "'Bats' Belfree." He sighed. "He's a nice enough guy, but one of the worst salesmen you'll ever meet."

"Would you say he's honest?" questioned Frank.

Claypool grinned. "Too honest," he replied. "When you're a CompuCar salesman, you don't tell customers that our CC-2000 is overpriced."

"Is it?" asked Joe.

Claypool leaned close to Joe, and in a conspiratorial whisper, he said, "It used to be, but since all those freaky accidents at the factory, the cost of producing these cars has gone up. Stockard hasn't raised the sticker price yet, but if the accidents continue, who knows? We may have to raise our prices or we'll go out of business.

"Anyway," Claypool continued, "here are the keys to your own CC-2000. After you drive it around, you can decide for yourself if it's worth the sticker price. Maybe you'll even want to buy one after you finish your work for Mr. Stockard. I'll give you a good price," he added.

"I can see that *you're* a good salesman," Joe said with a smile. "But we've got a van back home that just needs a little work. I think we'll be keeping it. Right, Frank?"

Frank looked at the sticker price on the

CC-2000's window and gave a low whistle. "You bet we'll keep the van. I can't believe the price of this car!"

"Actually, it's a bargain at that price," said Gil Claypool. "You'll see what I mean when you drive it. Come on, let's program in both of your voice patterns so that the car will respond to either one of you."

After Frank and Joe were given a quick lesson on how to drive the computer-operated CC-2000, the showroom's bay doors were opened and the Hardys roared out onto the street. It had stopped drizzling and, with Frank at the wheel, they followed Gil Claypool's directions to the CompuCar factory. The factory was located in an industrial park outside of Bayport.

"How about testing our new super wheels," Joe suggested. "Let's turn on the radio."

"Good idea." Frank punched the button on the steering wheel and said, "We want the radio turned on to the strongest FM rock 'n' roll station that's playing a song. Skip any station that's on a commercial."

As soon as Frank finished speaking, the radio flipped on, and a hit song poured out of the car's front and rear speakers.

18

"You don't happen to have a lot of extra money lying around I can borrow?" asked Joe. "This car is fantastic!"

Frank laughed and said, "Let's enjoy the car while we've got it. But how about starting to work on this sabotage case, too?" He glanced at his brother. "What did Claypool say about the falling beam?"

"He thinks it was just an accident," Joe replied. "He said the workers up there are pretty careless. What did you find out from Belfree?"

Frank filled his brother in on the fired employee's claim that Arnold Stockard had plenty of enemies. He passed along the names of Robert Blane and Alan Krisp, the two men whom Stockard had supposedly cheated out of their share of the company.

"Nice guy, Stockard," was Joe's comment.

"But we can't be sure Belfree is telling the truth," said Frank. "Remember, he's a guy with a grudge against his former boss."

"Well, I hope we can find some useful clues when Stockard shows us around the factory," said Joe. "So far, we don't have much to go on."

"Be patient," said Frank. "We're just getting started." He grinned at his brother. "Anyway, the longer we're on this case, the more we get to drive around in this car!"

Joe was about to comment on the new case—and new car—when both of them were alerted by the sudden electronic buzz of the car phone.

"Who could be calling us?" Joe wondered aloud.

"Maybe it's Gil Claypool," offered Frank. "He's the only one who would know the car's telephone number."

"Makes sense," said Joe. He picked up the phone and said, "Hello?"

At first, Joe thought he heard a small explosion of air on the other end. Then a voice began to speak.

Joe listened in silence for a few moments to the raspy voice on the other end of the line.

Then there was a click and the line went dead. The caller had hung up. Joe replaced the phone and took a deep breath.

"Well, who was it?" asked Frank.

Joe calmly turned to his brother and said, "Just somebody who wants to kill us."

3 Bugged!

"What!" exclaimed Frank, jerking his head toward his brother. He saw Joe's cool, serious expression. "You're not kidding, are you?" asked Frank.

"I never kid about things like that." Then Joe told him what the caller had said.

"Here it is, word for word," said Joe. "He said: 'I know what you're up to. I give you fair warning. Stay away from CompuCar, or you'll die.'"

The Hardys drove along in silence for a few moments before Frank spoke the thought that was on both of their minds: "It looks like that falling beam wasn't an accident, after all."

"But only two people knew we were coming to the showroom—Gil Claypool and Arnold Stockard," countered Joe, trying to put the pieces of the mystery together. "Claypool was inside the showroom right after the beam fell, so obviously he couldn't have been up on the roof. And we both saw Stockard drive away to his meeting."

"There's another possibility," said Frank.

"I'm sitting on the edge of my bucket seat. What is it?"

"The only answer that makes sense is that Arnold's Stockard's car phone was bugged. Our death threat caller must have learned that we were hired when Stockard called ahead to tell Claypool we were coming."

"Right," Joe quickly agreed. "In the time it took for Stockard to drop us off to pick up our car, our friend on the phone set up that so-called accident in front of the showroom. Whoever we're up against is playing rough," Joe added in a soft voice. "That steel beam might have been just a warning—like the phone call. But it could have killed us."

"You're right about that," Frank said thoughtfully, "but now we just might have something to work with. If there really is a bug in Stockard's car, we can use it to feed false information to the saboteur."

"I like it," said Joe. "When we get to the factory, we'll find Stockard's car. Then we'll tell the saboteur something that will flush him out into the open. And then we'll nail him. Simple as that."

"Yeah, simple as that—but only if we're right and Stockard's car is really bugged."

While they were talking, they cruised down a busy street that was just a few miles away from the CompuCar factory. Now that they had a plan, Frank and Joe were anxious to put it into action.

But the action started before they were ready.

A black sedan with dark, tinted windows zoomed up behind them and slammed into their rear bumper. Taken completely by surprise, Frank lost control of the CC-2000!

The car skidded off to the right, and the passenger side wheels jumped the curb. A mailman on the sidewalk leapt out of the way. Frank hit the brakes and the car skidded toward a telephone pole. The only thing Frank could do was jerk the wheel to his left, bringing the car back into the street. The rear of the CC-2000 fishtailed when it hit the pavement and the car suddenly went into a spin. The other cars on the street swerved to get out of the way.

Frank and Joe ended their spin on the wrong side of the street. Their engine had shut down and a truck was barreling toward them, the driver frantically blowing his horn. He couldn't stop in time, and there was no place he could turn to avoid the stalled CC-2000 blocking the road.

Frank didn't know what else to do except to punch the button on the steering wheel and shout, "Get us out of here!"

The CC-2000 motor immediately jumped to life, and the car lurched off the road. Frank quickly steered into a nearby empty driveway. An instant later, the truck screamed past them, missing their car by less than two inches.

Frank, drained from the ordeal, slumped forward. As a joke, just to relieve the tension, he absently touched the button on the steering wheel again and whispered, "Thanks."

"You're welcome," answered the CC-2000's electronic voice.

Frank and Joe saw no sign of the black car that had rammed them. It had sped on ahead of them and was long out of sight by the time they were back on the road. But that didn't mean they had forgotten about it.

"You think the driver was the guy who called us on the car phone?" asked Frank.

"Well, it wasn't Aunt Gertrude," Joe replied with a grim smile.

"I just wish I had gotten a better look at that car," Frank said in a frustrated voice.

"It's too bad we couldn't get his license number."

"Are you serious?" asked Joe. "It happened too fast. You were lucky you saw the car at all."

A few minutes later, Frank and Joe pulled into the huge CompuCar factory parking lot. It was obvious that Stockard's assembly line was working at capacity because the lot was tightly packed with sedans and sports cars.

It was only the black sedans with tinted windows, though, that interested them. But there were just too many, and none of them showed any dents in the front. Besides, they didn't know if the car that had hit them had been dented. For that matter, they didn't even know if the black car had come here.

"Forget it," said Joe. "This isn't getting us anywhere. Let's go back to our original plan to find Stockard's car and see if it's bugged."

Reluctantly, Frank agreed and pulled into the visitors' parking area.

"Over there," said Joe, pointing, as they got out of their car. "Isn't that Stockard's CC-2000?"

The sleek CompuCar with the license plate "Boss 1" was sitting in a shady spot next to the wall of the main office area of the factory.

"That's it, all right," replied Frank. "Come on. Let's see if it's locked."

"Shouldn't we check in with Mr. Stockard first and let him know what we're doing?" asked Joe.

"Thought of that," Frank replied, "but if Stockard's car is bugged, his office might be, too. If we do this on our own, nobody will know what we're up to—including the saboteur."

They looked around to make sure they weren't being watched. Then Frank tried the door on the driver's side. They were in luck. It was unlocked.

"No talking," Frank cautioned in a whisper before sliding into the car. He reached over and opened the passenger side door. Joe hurried around, got in, and quickly—and quietly—closed the door behind him. If there really was a bug in the car, they didn't want the eavesdropper to know they were on to him.

Frank gingerly picked up the telephone receiver and opened it up, looking for a hidden listening device. At the same time, Joe leaned down under the dashboard and looked for any suspicious wires.

They found nothing—and that surprised them.

Slowly, carefully, they began to check the rest of the car.

After they had checked the ashtrays, the radio speakers, and had picked up the car's floormats, all without results, the Hardys sat back in frustrated silence. Where was the bug?

Then Frank gestured toward the glove compartment. It seemed like such an obvious place that Joe hadn't bothered opening it. But Frank was insistent. He mouthed the words "Glove compartment," and Joe gave in with a shrug, flipping the small storage area open. His eyes widened, but not because he had found a bug. Sitting in the glove compartment was a long white envelope marked *The Last Will and Testament of Frank and Joe Hardy*.

4 A Deadly Game

Joe took the envelope out of the glove compartment and handed it to his brother. Frank read the outside of the envelope, then ripped it open. Inside was a single piece of paper. He looked at it and then gave it to Joe. There were just three words neatly typed in the center of the sheet. It said: "I warned you."

There was no point in keeping quiet anymore. Frank and Joe knew that the saboteur had outfoxed them.

"This guy is smart," said Frank.

"Yeah, and he has a weird sense of humor, too," Joe added. "He sure scared me with that 'Last Will and Testament' routine. You don't think there'd be any fingerprints on that paper, do you? I mean, besides ours, that is?"

Frank shook his head. "No way. He's too

careful. But what I'd like to know is what he meant by 'I warned you.' I mean, it's all pretty elaborate—the envelope with our names on it, the message. But what's the payoff?"

Just then Joe said, "What's that sound?"

"What sound?" Frank asked.

"Listen."

They were both silent, straining their ears. It took a second, but soon they both heard something that sounded vaguely like ticking. They knew that the CC-2000 dashboard clock was a digital, so it didn't make any noise. But if it wasn't the car clock, then what could it be?

With a sickening realization, Frank and Joe knew exactly what it was—a time bomb!

"We've got to make a run for it," exclaimed Frank, reaching for the driver's side door.

Joe grabbed his brother's arm. "Wait," he cried. "We can't leave the car here with a bomb in it. We're right next to the factory. If the bomb goes off, it could blow up the whole side of the building. A lot of people inside could be hurt."

Frank let go of the door. "You're right," he admitted. "We've got to do something."

"You're good with cars," said Joe. "Can

you get the engine going? Then we can drive the car away from the factory and ditch it before the bomb goes off."

Frank shook his head. "There probably wouldn't be time for that. Anyway, you heard what Stockard said. The voice activation system on these cars makes them virtually impossible to steal."

"Then what are we going to do? Just sit here and talk until the car blows up?" There was a note of desperation in Joe's voice.

"No," Frank replied firmly. "We're going to look for that bomb and defuse it before it's too late . . . I hope," he added.

Fully aware that, at any second, the car might explode into a million pieces, the Hardys ripped the inside of the CC-2000 apart, looking first under the seats and inside the headrests. They even broke into the radio. That's when they found the bug, but it hardly mattered anymore. Their hearts were beating like crazy. Their time had to be nearly used up. But where was the bomb? Why couldn't they find it?

"We've got to think like the saboteur," said Frank. "He likes to play games. The phone call, the bug in the radio, the Last Will and Testament—they're games. He's playing with us."

30

"Okay," Joe said. "So where would a saboteur with a sense of humor put a ticking time bomb?"

At the same instant, both Frank and Joe Hardy shouted, "It's behind the digital clock!"

They quickly smashed the front of the car's timepiece and found exactly what they were looking for. There, on a small shelf inside the dashboard next to the inner workings of the digital clock, was a mass of intricate wires heading to a small, ticking package. But the most frightening thing they saw was the wristwatch-sized clock that sat on top of the explosive. The clock showed that the bomb would go off in just fifty-five seconds!

They had less than a minute to figure out how to defuse it.

"I've never seen a bomb like that before," said Frank. "I don't know what wires to pull. Do you?"

Joe swallowed hard. "It's a mystery to me, too," he replied, discouraged. But then he took a deep breath. At least they'd found the bomb. That meant there was hope.

Fifty seconds left.

"That wire on the top," said Joe, carefully pointing. "It looks like it leads away from the bomb—maybe to a power source. If we cut that wire, maybe we'll defuse the bomb."

"Or automatically set it off," said Frank, uncertain that Joe was right.

Forty seconds left.

"All right," conceded Joe. "What about that small red wire that's connected to the clock? If we rip that out, it just might stop the timer. How about it?"

"I don't know," said Frank, shaking his head. "This is such a sophisticated bomb, pulling one single wire may not be enough to defuse it."

Thirty seconds left.

"Come on, Frank," Joe pleaded. "We can't debate this all day. We've got to make a decision," he insisted as he nervously watched the second hand move down to the twenty-five-second mark. When Frank didn't answer him, Joe threw up his hands in exasperation and said, "If you can't make up your mind, maybe we should pull all of the wires!"

Frank blinked. "That's it!" he cried.

"What? What did I say?"

"We'll pull all the wires at exactly the same time," Frank explained. "That way, even if we pull the wrong ones, it won't matter. But the key is to make sure we pull all of them at the same time."

"You're serious?"

"I'm betting our lives on it."

"Yeah, you're serious, all right," Joe said with a frown.

Fifteen seconds left.

Carefully, making sure not to upset the small but deadly package of explosives, Frank and Joe each wrapped their fingers around every wire sticking out of the bomb.

Ten seconds left.

"Ready?" asked Frank in a tense whisper.

"Wait. Let me get a better grip."

"When I say 'Now,' we pull. And don't hesitate," warned Frank.

Precious moments passed.

"Okay. Whenever you're ready," said Joe, sweat pouring down his face.

The clock ticked off the final seconds. Four . . . three . . . two . . .

"Now!"

Frank and Joe yanked as hard as they could, tearing each and every wire out of the bomb at the very same moment. The Hardy brothers held their breath as the clock ticked another beat—and then stopped, not moving, with just one second left.

The bomb was defused.

The two brothers heaved the biggest sigh of relief in the history of Bayport.

When Frank and Joe entered the factory, they stopped at the reception desk. The gum-chewing receptionist stared at the bomb in Frank's hands. She made a quick call upstairs. Then, she gave them both passes and directions to Arnold Stockard's office, on the seventh floor.

A secretary was sitting at a desk outside Stockard's office. A name card on the desk said "Ms. Cynthia Cooke."

"Here," said Frank, handing the time bomb to Ms. Cooke. "Please have this sent to Detective Con Riley at the Bayport Police Station. Tell him that Frank and Joe Hardy would like his expert opinion as soon as possible on how this bomb was put together."

Cynthia Cooke's eyes widened at the mention of the word *bomb*. "Oh, no," she said. "Where did you find it?"

"In Mr. Stockard's car," answered Frank.

"Oh, no. Oh, no," the secretary repeated, tears forming in her eyes. "Now it's bombs. Sabotage wasn't enough. This is terrible. None of us is going to be safe here."

"Well, we hope you're wrong about that," said Frank. "In fact, that's why we're here.

Mr. Stockard is expecting us. Frank and Joe Hardy."

"Yes, I know," said the secretary apologetically, "but he was called into a very important meeting." She leaned forward and whispered, "He's meeting with his insurance agent. Mr. Stockard's going to collect plenty with all these accidents. And he's going to need every penny to keep the company going. The sabotage has cost CompuCar a fortune!" she explained.

"How long will we have to wait for him?" asked Joe.

"Oh," Ms. Cooke said, brightening. "You don't have to wait for him. He wants you to go right to work. He's asked Edward Hartman, our computer engineer, to show you around the factory. In fact, Mr. Hartman should be here any second now because I buzzed him the minute the receptionist announced you."

Then she smiled and leaned forward again, whispering, "You're going to like Mr. Hartman. He's an absolute genius with those computers. And he'll give you a much better tour than Mr. Stockard would. Frankly"— the whisper got even softer—"Mr. Hartman knows much more about this company than Mr. Stockard does. I'm not kidding. He's really a genius. You'll see."

"Hello there!" said a booming voice. Frank and Joe looked toward the doorway to the hall and saw a pudgy man with a ready smile coming toward them. He was wearing a gray suit, a bright yellow bow tie, and horn-rimmed glasses.

"Oh, Mr. Hartman," Cynthia Cooke gushed. "I didn't see you come in."

"Well, here I am, nonetheless," he replied cheerfully. "And you two," he said, gesturing toward Frank and Joe, "must be the young detectives I've heard about from Mr. Stockard. I must say, I'm rather glad that Arnold was too busy to give you the tour. Otherwise," he explained, "I might not have had the honor of meeting you."

As Frank and Joe shook hands with Edward Hartman, the computer specialist looked past them and noticed the time bomb. "Excuse me," he said, "but what is that machine on Cynthia's desk?"

"It's an explosive device," answered Frank. "You might as well know, we found it in Mr. Stockard's car."

Hartman shook his head in despair. "What is this world coming to," he muttered. "Well, in any event," he continued, with a cheerful smile, "it's a good thing you found it when you did, right?"

36

"You can say that again," said Joe with a lopsided grin directed at his brother.

"Well, then," Mr. Hartman announced. "I suppose I ought to do what I was sent here for, which is to give you a tour of the factory."

"And specifically," added Frank, "the places where the previous sabotage took place."

"Of course," said Hartman. "Let's be on our way."

Edward Hartman led them down a long corridor toward the assembly line. As they walked down the hallway, employees looked up from their desks and smiled and waved at the dapper Hartman. He was quick to wave back and call out a few words of encouragement. He was evidently well liked by the CompuCar employees.

"A lot of people work here," Joe noted.

"Yes," agreed Hartman. "CompuCar employs exactly one thousand two hundred and eleven people. But you haven't seen anything yet. Wait until we reach the assembly line."

True to his word, when they came to the end of the hallway and turned left, they entered a cavernous room the size of three football fields. The place was humming with activity. Everywhere Frank and Joe looked there were conveyor belts carrying CC-2000s in different stages of production. Some of the cars had no doors, others had no wheels, still others were without bumpers. And all around the conveyor belts, choking the walkways, were hundreds of busy assembly line workers. But to Frank and Joe, the most amazing thing of all were the thousands of robots doing the heavy lifting and the dangerous welding work. It was an awesome sight.

"Those robots are amazing," said Joe, watching with fascination as two metal arms picked up a tire and then shoved it onto a wheel.

Hartman grinned. "Every robot in this factory is controlled by my computer programs. The conveyor belts, the lights, the heat and air conditioning—everything is tied into the factory's computer system."

"I'm impressed," said Frank with sincerity.

"Me, too," Joe chimed in. "I guess if you've got a computer-operated car, it makes sense that the factory that builds the cars is computer-operated, too."

"Exactly," said Hartman, pleased that his

two guests appreciated his accomplishments.

The computer genius then led them to an idle conveyor belt. "It's broken beyond repair," he announced. "Sabotage."

"What happened?" asked Frank.

"Good question. We're not quite sure. All we know is that when we came to work last Tuesday morning, the motor for this belt had literally melted!"

"Can I look at it?" asked Joe.

"Of course." Hartman asked an employee to take the metal panel off the motor casing. Joe peered inside and saw nothing but a lump of gray.

"You weren't exaggerating," said Joe. "It looks like metal pudding."

Meanwhile, Frank was exploring the immediate area, looking for clues, trying to figure out how the saboteur had caused the motor to overheat to the point of meltdown. He examined the motor casing and the wiring, noting that none of it had been damaged. That's strange, he thought. How could a motor get so hot without the electrical system being affected? It was a puzzle.

"I'll show you the spare parts area next," said Hartman, taking them on a route along the back wall of the factory, past circuit boards and switches, until they reached a massive pile of rusty, corroded carburetors.

"What's this?" asked Frank, confused.

"More sabotage," replied Hartman. "We make our own special carburetors here at the factory, and we keep them here until they're needed on the assembly line.

"Well," he continued, "just this morning, I came in and found all of our brand-new carburetors had been somehow chemically treated and had aged into junk, virtually overnight! And without those carburetors, we have to temporarily stop all production. It's a terrible blow."

While they were on their way to the next sabotage site, Frank saw someone dart behind a robot. When they walked past another aisle, he caught a glimpse of the same shadowy figure moving along after them, keeping them in view.

"We've got company," Frank whispered to Joe. "When we hit the next aisle, glance to your right. You'll see him tracking us."

Joe did as his brother suggested and, sure enough, he caught sight of someone who was obviously spying on them.

"That's pretty suspicious behavior," Joe said softly so that only Frank could hear him. "What do you want to do?"

"Before we reach the next aisle, you fall

40

back. Make an excuse so you don't alarm Hartman. He might get nervous and mess up our plan. Then race down the aisle we just passed and circle behind the spy. When I yell your name, try to grab him. I'll come at him from this end. If we're lucky, we'll sandwich this guy."

"Did you say something?" asked Hartman, turning back to Frank and Joe.

"I was just telling my brother to go on ahead," said Joe quickly. "I think I've got something in my shoe. I'll catch up to you."

Hartman nodded and continued to lead the way. When they reached the next aisle, Frank saw the spy's back foot as he lurched behind a pillar. They didn't know who he was or why he was following them—but they intended to find out. And they were going to find out right now!

5 Alan Krisp

"Joe!" shouted Frank Hardy, his voice thundering above the roar of the assembly line machinery.

The two brothers ran at top speed, from two different directions, toward someone who obviously didn't want to be caught. The man who had been lurking in the shadows bolted, racing down another aisle. Then, just when Joe was about to tackle him, the man jumped over a low conveyor belt out of his reach.

But Frank was closing in on him from the other side of the aisle.

The assembly line workers had stopped to watch the pursuit.

The man Frank and Joe were after was quick. But he was an older man and his age finally began to catch up with him—and so did the Hardys.

42

As Frank closed in on him, with Joe not far behind, the man looked wildly down one aisle and then another, trying to decide which way to run.

He made the wrong choice, turning down an aisle that was suddenly blocked by a robot arm reaching down to pick up an engine block. Like a metal bar coming down at a railroad crossing, the robot arm stopped the man dead in his tracks. He whirled around toward Frank and Joe.

The two brothers expected him to try and fight his way past them. But instead the man simply stopped. He leaned against the side of a conveyor belt and held his hands up in front of his body as if the Hardys were holding a gun on him.

"I give up," he wheezed, unable to catch his breath.

"Who are you and why were you following us?" demanded Frank, his hands balled into fists in case the man tried to make another run for it.

"I . . . I'm Alan . . . Alan Krisp," he answered breathlessly. "And I . . . I wasn't following you," he claimed.

"That's a lie," Joe said heatedly. "If you weren't following us, then why did you run away?"

"I don't know. . . . I guess I panicked. I saw you charging at me . . . and I just got scared, so I ran."

"Sure," said Joe skeptically. "And I'm the President of the United States."

"Listen," said Krisp, looking up and down the aisle to see who was in earshot, "I'm telling you the truth. Please believe me. I—"

Suddenly Krisp shut up like a clam. Edward Hartman hustled into view, shouting, "What's going on here? What's happening? Is that you, Alan?"

"Yes, it's me, Edward," Krisp said dully. "There's been some kind of misunderstanding," he sputtered. "These two suddenly attacked me, for no reason, and I ran."

"Just a minute!" Joe said with indignation. "That's not how it was, and you know it!"

Hartman put his hand on Joe's shoulder to calm him down. "Now, now," he said. "I'm sure Alan had a perfectly good reason for his actions. Isn't that right?"

The two men stared at each other, their eyes locked in a cold expression. It was Krisp, however, who finally looked away.

"I guess I'll be going back to my job, now," said Krisp without emotion.

"Yes, you do that, Alan. And in the future," Hartman added, "please try not to make a spectacle of yourself in front of the employees. It's bad for morale."

Krisp said nothing. He merely turned and walked away.

"Tell us about Alan Krisp," Frank insisted when the man was out of sight.

A pained look creased Hartman's face. "Alan Krisp and a friend of his used to own half of CompuCar—until Arnold Stockard pulled a rather clever legal maneuver and took over complete control of the company."

"And Alan wasn't too happy about it, right?" questioned Frank.

"You could put it that way," Hartman said with a grimace. "But in all fairness, Mr. Stockard did give Alan a job here, allowing him to stay on to oversee the new car body production."

Frank remembered what the fired showroom salesman, Belfree, had said about Stockard and his business methods. He also remembered that Alan Krisp's name had been mentioned. It was more than an interesting coincidence. "This Alan Krisp must be a pretty bitter man," probed Frank.

Hartman narrowed his eyes and replied, "Alan isn't the only person around here that Stockard's taken advantage of.

"But," he quickly added, forcing a smile, "that's business. Some people fail and others succeed. It's the way of the world."

"As far as I'm concerned," said Joe, "this guy Krisp could be our saboteur. He's got a motive, and the fact that he was sneaking around, following us, makes him look pretty guilty."

"Yes," admitted Hartman. "I can see where you might think that, but you don't have any proof. And while Alan and I obviously don't get along, I must tell you that I don't believe he's the man you're after."

"Then who is?" asked Frank.

Edward Hartman laughed. "If I knew that," he said, "Mr. Stockard wouldn't have called on you."

"Well, there must be a few people you suspect, Mr. Hartman," Frank prodded. "After all, you know the people who work here. We don't. If you can give us a lead or two, maybe we can track down this saboteur and have him thrown in jail."

"Perhaps," said Hartman softly. "But I'm afraid I don't know the people here as well as you think I do. Oh, I get along with the employees well enough," he added, "but I don't really understand why people do the things they do. Me, I understand computers. Come on, I'll show you."

They followed him down a long corridor, but Hartman stopped at a water cooler. "I'll be just a moment," he said, digging into his jacket pocket. His hand came out holding a small bottle of vitamin C. He popped two of the pills in his mouth and took a drink of water.

"I have a cold coming on," he explained. "I should have mentioned it before. I always try to warn people ahead of time; I hate being responsible for causing anyone an illness that could have been avoided."

"We'll keep our distance," said Frank. "Thanks for the tip."

"Think nothing of it," Hartman said with a smile.

He then continued down the hall to a computer work station. "I do most of my computer work in my lab upstairs, but I sometimes dabble down here," he explained, as he hit a quick series of keys on the keyboard. The words "What is your command?" flashed on the computer monitor.

Hartman turned to Frank and Joe and announced, "With just the touch of a few keys, we can change anything on the assembly line. You decide. What should we do? Speed up the door handle welding? Have the car radios set to your favorite rock station? What's your choice?"

"I noticed that at the end of the assembly line you only fill the cars up with one gallon of gas," said Frank. "How about adding an extra gallon? After all, the car costs so much money. Why not be a sport?"

Hartman shrugged, but his eyes twinkled behind his glasses. "Mr. Stockard won't like it, but let's do it." He hit a few keys, then typed out the words *two gallons*.

The assembly line slowed down to allow for the extra gassing up of the cars.

"That was too easy," the computer genius said. "Give the factory computer another test. Anything at all," he challenged.

"If all these cars are programmed to talk," said Joe, "how about making them say the same thing at the same time?"

"But of course," said Hartman with a grin as he typed a new command onto the computer keyboard.

A moment later, every car on the assembly line suddenly blurted out "Hello" in a chorus of electronic voices.

"I love these demonstrations." Hartman chortled. "It always amazes my guests when they see how much a computer can really do."

Frank nodded his head. "We have a computer at home and I do a little tinkering with it," he said modestly. "But you've obviously got your computers hooked up to absolutely everything on the factory floor. It's really remarkable."

"Thank you. I'm very proud of what I've done here. Very proud," he repeated. "Now, then, can I show you anything else?"

Joe glanced around the busy factory, seeing the workers frantically trying to keep up with the fast-moving assembly line. "How about stopping everything for ten minutes to give everyone a rest?" he suggested.

"Hmmm." Hartman contemplated the request, then glanced at his watch. "Mr. Stockard might be upset at the lost productivity," he finally said, "but our employees are supposed to get a scheduled break in about half an hour. I suppose, though, that we could give it to them now. Okay," he agreed. "I just need to type in a few—"

Before Hartman could type the command onto the keyboard, every light in the factory suddenly went off. The factory was plunged into total darkness!

6 Blackout!

When the lights went out there were cries of surprise throughout the pitch-dark factory. The assembly line, the robots, everything was still moving—but nobody could see what was happening!

Soon the cries of surprise turned to screams of panic, as the workers accidentally walked into robot arms that hit them and knocked them down. They stumbled into conveyor belts. Open car doors on the assembly line were snapped off when they hit pillars farther down the line. Crunching metal and broken window glass flew in every direction.

The factory was in chaos.

"It's the saboteur!" cried Edward Hartman from somewhere behind Frank and Joe.

"Do you have a flashlight up here?" Frank asked Hartman.

"As a matter of fact, I do have a small one," replied Hartman, opening a drawer. "Ah, here it is," he said, placing the flashlight in Frank's hands. "Such a simple tool, but very handy in a crisis."

Frank tested the flashlight. It didn't give off much light, but it was better than nothing.

"Do you remember seeing a circuit breaker during our tour?" Frank called out to his brother.

"Yeah," Joe answered over the screams of the workers. "It was on the far wall."

"Think we can find it again?"

"We can sure try," said Joe with his usual pluck.

Frank and Joe left Hartman in his office and made their way carefully down to the factory floor.

"Are we going in the right direction?" Frank asked as they headed down an aisle. "The beam of the flashlight is so weak, I can't tell."

"I think so," replied Joe. "We were facing the right way when the lights went out, and I never turned around. This aisle ought to take us to the wall. When we get there, I'll head in one direction and you go in the other. One of us will eventually find the circuit breaker."

51

But first they bumped into an assembly line worker who had fallen down and was lying across the aisle. Frank lost his balance and tripped over the man's outstretched legs, hitting the floor with a heavy thud.

"Frank? You okay?" Joe called out in alarm.

"Just bumped my head," he replied. "Nothing serious." He crawled around to the person he had fallen over, shined the flashlight on his face, and asked if he was all right.

"Just fine," replied the man, who looked to be in his early sixties. "I figure I'm safer down here than up there walking around." He added, "The way I see it, I can't fall if I'm already on the floor."

"Good thinking," said Frank with a grin, patting the man on the shoulder. "But why don't you move over a little so nobody else falls on top of you? That way, you'll be even safer."

"You got it," said the man, sliding over next to the conveyor belt.

Shakily, Frank got to his feet. "Let's keep going," he said to his brother. "But watch out. You never know who you're going to step on."

They gingerly made their way down the aisle without any problems. Then, the assembly line sent a two-ton car chassis hurtling sideways off the conveyor belt. It crashed to the floor right in front of them with an ear-splitting boom and rolled over away from them, landing on its roof.

"We've got to find that circuit breaker and get the lights on," Frank said. "This place is falling apart!"

"The wall can't be that much farther," Joe answered. "Just keep going."

They had to climb over the wrecked car in the aisle, but they were relieved when they reached the wall just a few short strides later.

"I'll go to my right," said Joe. "You got to the left. And Frank?"

"Yeah?"

"As soon as we get the lights back on, let's find Alan Krisp. I've got a sneaky suspicion he wasn't where he was supposed to be when these lights went out."

"I was thinking the same thing. If Hartman and Stockard need proof, let's get it for them."

"Right."

They each went in separate directions. Joe had insisted that his brother keep the flashlight. Now Joe inched his way along the wall, feeling for the circuit breaker he knew had to be somewhere nearby. He found a soda machine, a painting, which he almost knocked off the wall, and an awful lot of empty space.

Frank also found a lot of empty space along the wall, until the flashlight showed him a metal box. The circuit breaker!

He fumbled around the edge of the cover until he finally got it open. As soon as he had his fingers on the switches inside the box, he started pulling them like a madman.

At first nothing happened. Then, a few seconds later, the lights finally flickered on.

A huge cheer went up in the factory. The disaster was over.

But Frank and Joe weren't content with simply stopping the saboteur's latest attack on the CompuCar Company. They wanted to catch him and stop him from ever doing it again. With that thought in mind, they both went in search of their number-one suspect, Alan Krisp.

Joe was the first one to find him. It didn't take very long. Krisp was sitting at a corner desk at the far end of that same wall.

"I'll ask you my question first," Joe said, interrupting Krisp, who was talking to a man in a trench coat who stood nearby. "Then I'll ask the people around you. So you'd better tell the truth."

54

"About what?" asked Krisp, raising his eyebrows in surprise.

"Where were you when the lights went out?" Joe demanded.

Krisp looked perplexed. Then he grinned. "You don't think I did that, do you?"

"That's exactly what I think," said Joe, nodding grimly. He added, "You're in a perfect place to have done it, too. It would have been easy for you to throw the switches in the circuit box and then just follow the wall right back here to your desk. Almost anybody else would have had to make his way through the assembly line—and let me tell you, that wouldn't have been easy."

"What you're saying makes perfect sense," Krisp conceded easily, "but your conclusion is wrong. I didn't cause the blackout. I was here the entire time."

Frank finally caught up to his brother. He had heard enough to come up with a pointed question of his own.

"You claim you didn't cause the blackout," he said. "But if you admit it would have been easy to move along the wall to the circuit breaker, why didn't you try to turn the lights back on once they were off?"

Krisp's face turned bright red. "I . . . uh . . . didn't think of it," he mumbled.

"Or maybe you were enjoying the panic you had created," countered Joe.

"That's ridiculous." Krisp fumed. "I tell you, I was here the whole time."

"That's what you say," said Joe. Then the younger Hardy brother turned to the man in the trench coat and asked, "Were you here before the blackout?"

"Yes, I was," said the man.

"And was Alan Krisp here when the lights went out?"

The man paused for a second, looked at Krisp with a knowing smile, and then replied, "Yes. He was here the entire time."

Frank saw the look that had passed between the two men, and he wondered what it meant. "What's your name?" he asked the man in the trench coat.

"Blane," he replied. "Robert Blane. And who are you two to be asking all these questions?"

Before either of them could answer, Alan Krisp said, "They're Frank and Joe Hardy, the young detectives Stockard asked to find the saboteur. Hartman was showing them around."

"Hartman, huh?"

Krisp nodded.

The man in the coat squinted his eyes at Frank and Joe and shook his head. "Well, if

56

you think Alan here is the saboteur, you're barking up the wrong tree."

"We didn't say he was," countered Frank. "We're only saying that he could be. By the way," Frank added thoughtfully, remembering what the fired showroom salesman had said earlier about Blane and Krisp, "didn't you and Mr. Krisp once own the CompuCar Company together until Stockard forced you to sell?"

"Who told you that?" demanded Blane. "Was it Hartman?"

"As a matter of fact, it wasn't," Frank said coolly.

"Then who was it? I'm sure it wasn't Stockard," he shot back confidently.

"It doesn't matter who told us," Joe said, stepping into the discussion. "What matters is whether or not it's true. And if it is, then you're just as good a suspect as Mr. Krisp."

"That's hogwash," said Blane haughtily. "You don't have any proof that I'm involved with this sabotage business. Yes, it's true that Alan and I were once partners with Stockard," he went on. "You could easily check the facts. And, yes, it's true that he bought us out of our share of the company for peanuts just before it started making money. But that doesn't mean that either one of us wants to destroy Stockard. I admit,

I felt cheated at first. That's why I left CompuCar, but Alan was content to stay on as an employee, and I'm perfectly happy in my new business. In fact, I prefer it. Of course, I do have a lot of feelings about CompuCar and the people who work here. In fact, I have very strong feelings."

"Strong enough to bring you here just at the time there's a blackout?" questioned Frank.

Blane shifted uncomfortably. "I had no way of knowing that there was going to be a blackout. I simply came here to drop something off with an old friend," he said, indicating Alan Krisp with a nod of his head. "And neither Alan nor I had anything to do with the blackout or any of the other acts of sabotage that have plagued this factory.

"My advice to you, young man," Blane added disdainfully, "is to leave innocent, law-abiding people like Alan and myself alone, and use your brains—if you have any—to find the real culprit. Frankly, it shouldn't be too hard—although finding the *proof* might be difficult," he said, surprising Frank with those final words.

Was Blane daring them to prove that he was the saboteur? Or was he suggesting that he knew who the saboteur was, but wouldn't —or couldn't—say? Frank was confused.

And Frank couldn't help but wonder if maybe that was just what Blane wanted.

While Frank and Blane talked, Joe quietly sidled over to look at something that had caught his eye on Alan Krisp's desk. It was a colorful travel brochure for Rio de Janeiro, in Brazil.

It looked to Joe as if Krisp was planning a trip. And, curiously, it was a trip to a South American country that was outside the authority of the U.S. police, even the FBI. That meant that if Krisp broke the law in America and fled to Rio, he couldn't be arrested and brought back to the United States.

Krisp, unaware of Joe's lingering glance at his desk, rose to his feet in exasperation, saying, "I'm tired of all these suspicions against me and Bob. In fact, I'm just plain tired. I'm going home. And I think I'll call in sick tomorrow."

Krisp hurriedly gathered some papers from his desk—including the brochure for Rio—and stuffed them into his briefcase. "Someday," he said, this time looking at Blane rather than Frank and Joe, "the identity of the saboteur will be known. But I doubt very much that you two," he said, swinging his gaze around to the Hardys, "will find him before he's done his worst."

Was that a challenge? wondered Frank

59

and Joe, as Alan Krisp and Robert Blane sauntered out of the CompuCar factory.

Joe told his brother about the travel brochure to Rio.

"If he's our man," Frank said, "then we may not have much time to catch him."

"Krisp could be working with Blane," Joe suggested. "We haven't considered that this might be the work of more than one person. That would explain how the saboteur seems to get around so fast. I mean, he—or they—were listening to bugs, dropping steel beams on our head, running us off the road, setting a time bomb, and causing a blackout, all in one day."

"Yeah," said Frank. "And the day isn't over yet. But you could be right about those two guys. Maybe they're working together. We'd better check it out."

"Okay. And the first thing we should do is find out if they have alibis for all the other acts of sabotage," said Joe.

"It would be very interesting," Frank added with a smile, "if it turned out that, as today, they're always giving alibis for each other."

"Well, let's get to work," said Joe. "We've got a lot of questions to ask."

But before they could start their investigation of Krisp and Blane, a voice over the factory loudspeaker boomed, "Will Frank and Joe Hardy please come to the reception area? You have a phone call."

"I wonder who it could be?" said Frank.

Joe shrugged and said, "Let's go find out."

A few minutes later, Frank picked up the receiver at the reception desk. "Hello, this is Frank Hardy," he said.

At the other end of the line, Detective Con Riley said urgently, "There's big trouble at the station. You'd better get down here right away. And I mean fast!"

7 Police Station Blues

"I wish Con hadn't been so quick to hang up," complained Frank as he backed their CC-2000 out of its parking spot and began the drive toward downtown. "I'd like to know why we've got to get to the station in such a hurry."

"It could be he looked at the time bomb and came up with something he didn't want to tell us over the phone," suggested Joe.

"It's possible. Anyway, I sure hope that's it."

As they put the CompuCar factory well behind them, Joe cleared his throat and said, "I've been thinking. It seems to me that both Krisp and Blane would have access to the sophisticated technology needed to put together that weird time bomb. Krisp is responsible for production of the company's car chassis, and it takes high-tech machinery to build high-tech chassis.

"And Blane," he went on, "was a co-owner of the CompuCar Company—which means he'd have had access to all their floor plans. He'd know the vulnerable points in the factory better than most—and he'd know just how to wreck the place."

"It could be either one of them or both of them," agreed Frank. "Or maybe neither one. Let's hope Con Riley has some answers for us when we get to the station."

"Guess you're right. No sense jumping to conclusions. Anyway, until we get to the station, how about listening to a little music?"

"Sure." Frank touched the button on the steering wheel and said, "Turn the radio on to WBAY."

They expected to hear their favorite rock station. Instead, the car's horn went off!

"What's going on? What's wrong?" demanded Joe.

"I don't know," said Frank, flustered. He hit the button on the steering wheel and shouted, "Turn off the horn!"

But it didn't do any good. The horn kept blaring. People in cars around them gave Frank and Joe dirty looks, thinking that they were causing the irritating sound on purpose.

"You've got to stop that horn," Frank

called out above the racket, "or we'll end up getting a ticket for disturbing the peace."

Frank reached again for the button on the steering wheel at the same time that Joe said, "Maybe the wires got crossed between the radio and the horn. If we turn off the radio—"

Suddenly, the horn stopped blaring.

"You did it," said Frank, laughing. "The car's computer heard you say 'turn off the radio.' You must have been right about the wires being crossed."

"Just lucky," Joe said. "But we played the radio on our way out here and the horn didn't go off. I wonder why it worked okay before and messed up now?"

"I'll tell you why," Frank said, taking a guess. "I'll bet this car is a lemon and Arnold Stockard knew it. He couldn't sell it, so he figured he'd lend it to us, instead."

"Based on what we've heard about the guy, I wouldn't be surprised," said Joe. "But with our van dead in its tracks, we're in no position to complain."

"Hey, you don't hear me saying we should trade in this CC-2000, do you? The car *did* save our lives just a few hours ago. So what if turning on the radio sets the horn blasting? We're smart, creative guys, right?"

"Right."

"And if we want some music, we know what to do. Right?"

"Right."

"So let's go ahead and do it. Right?"

"Right."

Frank hit the button on the steering wheel, looked over at his brother, and, together, they said, "Turn on the horn!"

A top-ten song immediately began playing on the radio.

"It worked!" cried Frank. "This CC-2000 is wild."

"You know, as soon as we get a chance, we ought to pick up Callie and Iola," Joe suggested, referring to Callie Shaw and Iola Morton, Frank and Joe's girlfriends. "They'd really love this car."

"They're not the only ones. Chet, Biff, and Tony wouldn't mind riding around the block in it, either. But business comes first," Frank said reluctantly.

"I hope Con Riley appreciates the fact that we're putting him ahead of our friends," Joe kidded.

Frank laughed and said, "He probably heard we were driving around town in this CC-2000, and he ordered us to the station so *he* could get a ride."

Nothing could have been further from the truth!

As soon as they arrived at Con Riley's office, the usually friendly detective jumped out of his chair and demanded, "What have you guys gotten yourselves into?"

"What do you mean?" asked Frank, stunned by the harsh greeting.

"What do I mean?" repeated Riley with an incredulous look on his face. "Remember that time bomb you sent down here?" he asked. The brothers nodded. "Well, for your information, it's the most scientifically advanced explosive device I've ever seen. But that's only part of the problem. The rest of the problem is that Chief Collig came into my office while I was looking at that bomb and—you'll pardon the expression—*he exploded!*"

"Why?" asked Joe guardedly.

"Well, first of all," said Riley, "he's not too crazy about the idea of sophisticated time bombs being discovered in Bayport. And second, he's even less crazy about the fact that he doesn't know what's going on. He wants to see the two of you right away."

"Thanks for the warning," said Frank.

"Sure," said the detective. "And, listen, I'm sorry I bit your heads off when you came in before, but the chief is really on the warpath."

The three of them left Riley's office and tramped down the hall to see Chief Collig. But before Riley opened the door, Frank stopped and asked him, "By the way, did you learn anything useful about the time bomb?"

"Only that you were lucky to have defused it. That was one complicated home-made bomb. I can tell you that it was no amateur who built it."

"Riley!" boomed a voice from the other side of the door. "Is that you?"

"Yes, Chief, it's me." Riley sighed.

"Are Frank and Joe Hardy with you?"

"Yes, they are."

"Then what are you waiting for?" Collig shouted. "Get them in here on the double!"

Riley looked at the Hardys and rolled his eyes. Then he swung open the door to the chief's office.

"It's good to see you, Chief," said Frank, holding out his right hand as he walked into the office.

Chief Collig was caught off guard by Frank's outstretched hand. He shook it, and then took Joe's hand and shook that, too.

"All right, you two," he said wearily. "Sit down and tell me what time bombs are doing in my town."

"Well, they're not going off," Joe said lightly, hoping to get a smile out of the chief.

No such luck.

"This is serious business, Joe," Collig replied evenly. "Your father is a friend of mine, and I wouldn't want to see you kids get hurt."

"We appreciate that, Chief," offered Frank. "And so far, we're just fine. No cuts, no bruises, no broken bones."

"I want to keep it that way," said Collig. "So why don't you tell me what you're up to and maybe I can help."

"I'd like to help, too," offered Con Riley, who was standing at the back of the room.

"We'll take all the help we can get," said Joe with a smile. "You guys have had a lot more experience than we've had."

"Since when did you become such a flatterer?" asked the chief warily.

"Since we heard you yelling outside the door," Joe admitted.

"Wise guy," said Collig. But just the same he laughed. "Tell me what's going on," he finally insisted.

Frank told Collig and Riley everything that had happened since they had met Arnold Stockard.

"Very interesting," said the chief when

Frank was finished. Con Riley suddenly stirred at the back of the room. "It looks like you've got an opinion on all this," Collig said generously. "Let's hear it."

"Based on what we've heard about Alan Krisp," suggested the detective, "I'd say that he looks like the prime suspect. I'd leave Robert Blane out of it, because the person we're looking for can get in and out of the CompuCar factory at will. Blane has his own business and just visits the factory from time to time."

"I was thinking the same thing," agreed Collig. "Let's run a check on Alan Krisp and see what we come up with. In the meantime, you sit tight," he added, turning toward Frank and Joe. "I'll get back to you after we see what we have in our computer files on Krisp."

The chief stood up.

"You watch how we catch that saboteur," he said boldly, showing Frank and Joe to the door. "You're going to see some good, old-fashioned police work. Maybe you'll even learn a thing or two."

Frank and Joe glanced at each other. Chief Collig was a good cop, but they felt they could solve this case themselves. After all, they had already provided the chief with their main suspect. All they had to do now was provide the chief with some proof.

"You ought to be a diplomat," Joe said as he and Frank climbed into their CC-2000. "We walked in there with Collig ready to read us the riot act, and we left with him giving us a pep talk. How do you do it?"

"Well, for one thing, I don't make jokes when somebody else is angry," he said, looking Joe straight in the eye.

"Okay, okay, maybe I could be a little more tactful," the younger Hardy brother admitted.

"That'll be the day," Frank said with a grin.

"Thanks for the encouragement," Joe kidded in return. "Now what do you say we get out of here and go home. I'm starving."

"Me, too," said Frank. "It's been a long time since breakfast!"

They drove down Main Street, passing Bayport's familiar shops and stores. It was rush hour and the driving was slow. While they waited at a light, Frank glanced in his rearview mirror.

"Uh-oh," he said ominously, gripping the steering wheel tightly.

"What is it?"

"Don't turn around," said Frank. "There's

a black sedan with dark tinted windows behind us. It looks a lot like the one that tried to run us off the road before."

"Can you make out the driver?" asked Joe, fighting the urge to turn and look for himself.

"No. I can't see his face. It's just a dark outline," said Frank, staring into the reflected image in the mirror. "But he looks like he's reaching for something. It's a telephone. He's got it to his ear and—"

The phone in the Hardys' car suddenly began to ring.

8 Stalking Two Suspects

Joe Hardy picked up the telephone expecting to hear the saboteur's raspy voice. But as soon as he lifted the receiver from its perch, the CC-2000's automatic door-locking mechanism went wild, locking and unlocking all four doors in a whirligig of motion. The incredibly rapid, constant clicking of the locks sounded almost like machine-gun fire.

Frank and Joe were so startled that they forgot about the black car behind them. But only until the sedan peeled out from behind them and zoomed up alongside the driver's side of the CC-2000.

Ignoring the snapping door locks, Frank was about to shout "Hold on!" to his brother, afraid that the driver of the other car was going to sideswipe them. But then he got a

72

good look inside the black car and saw a man talking on his car phone. He was waving one of his hands angrily, and it looked like he was shouting. Then he suddenly hung up. The guy in that car couldn't have cared less about Frank and Joe.

False alarm.

But that didn't end their crazy door-locking problem.

"This car is going bonkers again," Frank called out.

Joe figured that picking up the phone had started the problem, so hanging the phone up ought to stop it. To his surprise, that simple tactic didn't work. Instead, as soon as he hung up the phone, it started ringing again—and there was no one on the other end of the line.

"The wiring in this car is even more messed up than we figured," Joe complained.

"We've got to try something else," said Frank. He punched the button on the steering wheel, giving the car's computer all sorts of voice commands that neither stopped the ringing nor shut off the door-locking mechanism. To end the constant ringing, they finally just kept the phone off the hook. It wasn't until Frank commanded the car to turn on the rear window defogger that the door locks finally settled in the unlocked position.

"It looks like the electrical wiring—or something—is really messed up," said Joe. "But at least it isn't anything mechanical. At any rate, when we get finished with this CC-2000," he added, "we ought to tell Stockard to donate it to a theme park as a new attraction. They can call it the Car of a Thousand Surprises."

They made it home without any other problems, jumped out of the car, and hurried into the house.

"Do we have any potato chips?" asked Frank, rummaging around in the kitchen cabinets.

"Never mind the chips," said their mother. "I want you guys to sit down and eat a decent meal for a change."

They didn't need to be told twice. Laura Hardy was a great cook, and they devoured everything she put in front of them.

"I didn't know I had vacuum cleaners for sons," she kidded them. "Slow down and tell me about the case you're working on. Your father will want to hear all about it when he calls."

When they finished telling her everything, she nodded her head and said, "Sounds like an interesting case."

"Right now, all I'm interested in is what's for dessert," Joe said, grinning at his mother.

Laura Hardy smiled and disappeared into the kitchen. She returned carrying a cheesecake. "Your aunt Gertrude sent this by mail from New York," she said. "It arrived today."

The brothers' aunt Gertrude was Fenton Hardy's sister. She lived with the family, but at the moment, she was spending a month in New York City with friends.

"Aunt Gertrude definitely knows the right presents to send," Frank said as he cut into the cheesecake.

After dinner, the Hardy brothers helped their mother with the dishes. Then they watched a movie on TV. Before the movie was over, Frank had fallen asleep on the couch, and Joe was asleep in an easy chair. It had been a long day. They didn't even hear the phone ring, signaling Fenton Hardy's nightly call home.

Late the next morning, Frank headed for the den. There, Frank called Arnold Stockard with a progress report, including their theories concerning Alan Krisp and Robert Blane.

"Well, Alan certainly has the means," Stockard responded. "And, come to think of it, I did see Bob at the factory several times, just before the accidents started."

"He was there yesterday, during the blackout," Frank told him.

There was a short pause on the other end of the line. Then Stockard said, "If one or both of them is sabotaging *my* company, I want them caught. And I want proof. Understand?"

"We'll do our best, Mr. Stockard," Frank said quietly.

"Good," replied Stockard. Then there was a click and a dial tone. Stockard had hung up.

Frank gently replaced the receiver.

"What did he say?" Joe asked his brother.

"He wants proof," replied Frank.

"Then let's get it for him."

Frank nodded thoughtfully. "We need to talk to Krisp and Blane again," he said, reaching for the phone book. "Krisp said he was going to call in sick today, so he's probably at home."

Frank opened to the *K*s and ran his finger down a column. "Found him," he said. "Write this down. Alan Krisp lives at Thirty-seven Bellair Avenue."

"Got it," said Joe, scribbling the information on a piece of paper.

Frank leafed toward the front of the book

76

until he reached the *B*s. Scanning the columns, he finally called out, "Here's Blane. He's at Nineteen-oh-one McKelvey Road. His office is on the same street, but at Fifteen hundred McKelvey."

After Joe had taken down Blane's address, he said, "Let's see Krisp first. I want to find out more about that trip to Rio he's planning on taking."

"Good point," said Frank approvingly. "Let's go."

When the Hardy brothers left the house, Joe held out his hand and said, "Now it's my turn to drive our dream machine. You've had your fun."

Frank tossed his brother the car keys and said, "Be my guest. But if you think driving a lemon like that is fun, you're wrong. This dream machine is a nightmare!"

Joe got behind the wheel and started the car. He felt instantly at home. "Look out, Alan Krisp," he said. "Here we come."

As they drove along, Joe pulled an audio tape out of his shirt pocket and proudly held it up for Frank to see. "Knowing that the radio doesn't work," Joe announced, "I had the brains to bring along our own music."

"Well, don't say I didn't warn you when the deck chews up your tape," Frank replied with a knowing grin.

"Hey, with me in the driver's seat of this CompuCar, there isn't a thing to worry about. Trust me."

"I trust *you*," said Frank. "It's the *car* I don't trust."

Joe shrugged and put his tape into the cassette deck. Then he hit the special button on the steering wheel and said, "Let's hear some music on the deck, and no fooling around, car. Understand?"

The music played right on command— loud, sweet, and clear.

"Told you," said Joe, sporting a wide grin on his face. "You just have to let this car know who's boss, that's all. For instance, it's kind of stuffy in here." He hit the button on the steering wheel. "Car, open the windows halfway, immediately!"

Instead of the windows opening, Joe's audio tape came shooting out of the cassette deck like a bullet, leaving behind a trail of twisted tape.

Frank couldn't help it—he roared with laughter.

They arrived at Alan Krisp's house in the early afternoon with no further mishaps. Joe parked the car and the two of them hurried up the walk and rang Krisp's doorbell. There was no answer. Joe rang the bell again; then he knocked at the door. There was still no answer.

"Look at this," Joe said suddenly, pointing at a mailbox next to the door. The mailman had forgotten to close the lid. "The mail is still here. It seems our Mr. Krisp hasn't been home all morning."

Frank picked up the letters and magazines from the mailbox and rifled through them.

"Tampering with the mail is a federal crime," said Joe.

"I'm not tampering," corrected Frank. "I'm just peeking. Besides, didn't all that mail look like it was going to fall onto the ground? I'm just organizing it and putting it back so it won't get lost."

"You're a good citizen, Frank," Joe said with a straight face.

Frank paid no attention to Joe's sarcastic comment. His eyes were transfixed on one of the envelopes. "Here's something curious," he said, handing the letter to his brother.

It was an envelope addressed to Krisp from a major airline.

"Are you thinking what I'm thinking?" Joe asked.

"That there's a plane ticket to Rio in that envelope?"

"You're on my wavelength."

"We can't open it, though, because that

79

really would be tampering. Hold it up to the sun," suggested Frank.

That didn't help; they still couldn't read what was inside. Joe dumped all of Krisp's mail back in the mailbox. "This isn't getting us anywhere," he said, scratching his head. "We don't know if he's running away to Rio or not. All we know is that he called in sick but he isn't here."

"Then where is he?"

"He's friends with Robert Blane," said Joe. "So maybe Blane will know."

"Or maybe they're together," suggested Frank.

"Yeah, plotting the destruction of the CompuCar Company. We could catch them plotting their next accident at the factory. That would sure make things easy for us, wouldn't it?" said Joe.

"Come on, Joe, when have any of our cases ever been that easy?"

"Well, there's always a first time," Joe said hopefully.

When they got to Blane's house, they stood on the front porch, listening to the loud gong of the doorbell inside the house. When no one answered, Joe leaned in close to the door, hoping to hear the sound of footsteps coming in their direction. There were no footsteps, but he did hear the faint sound of a TV or radio.

"I think he's in there, but he won't open up," Joe declared.

"Let's find a window we can look through. Come on."

Frank led the way around the side of the house. Every window they saw had the blinds down or the curtains closed. Except for the kitchen window. It not only had its curtains open, the whole window itself was wide open. The only problem was that it was just slightly too high up off the ground to look into.

"Climb up on my shoulders," said Frank, leaning over.

Joe gingerly put first one foot, then the other, on his brother's back, precariously balancing himself as Frank slowly stood to his full height.

Joe grabbed the window ledge and pulled himself up. His eyes swept the room, seeing nothing out of the ordinary. He could hear the radio—he was sure that's what it was because he recognized the voice of a familiar deejay—and his gaze followed that sound into what was probably the living room.

His eyes widened in surprise, and he immediately began climbing in through the kitchen window.

"What are you doing?" demanded Frank in a harsh whisper. "You can't go in there!"

Joe didn't answer. He disappeared inside the house, not even bothering to stick his head out the window to tell Frank what he was up to.

Nearly a minute passed with Frank at a complete loss as to what was going on. Then, the back door swung open.

Joe stood there with a grim look on his face and said, "I just called the paramedics. Robert Blane is inside. So is Alan Krisp. They're both unconscious."

9 New Theories

One of the paramedics broke an ammonia capsule under Alan Krisp's nose. The strong, unpleasant odor made Krisp push the capsule away. His eyes fluttered open and he looked around without quite focusing. "Where is he?" Krisp asked woozily. "Where did he go?"

Frank leaned down over the shoulder of the paramedic. "Who are you talking about?" he asked. "Where did *who* go?"

"The . . . the man who hit me. The man who—" Suddenly his eyes opened wide. "Where's Bob? Is he all right?"

"He's right here, Mr. Krisp," offered Joe. "He's starting to come around, too. He'll be all right. But finish what you were saying," he insisted. "Who hit you?"

"I . . . I don't know," he said, gingerly touching the bump on the back of his head.

"Think," urged Frank. "Tell us what happened. Start from the beginning."

"I decided to take the day off, so I called in sick," Krisp admitted. "I left the house early and had breakfast out. Then I did some shopping for my trip." He looked up at Frank and Joe. "I'm going on vacation next week."

"To Rio de Janeiro?" interrupted Joe.

"No," he replied, surprised by the question. "Actually, I was thinking of Rio, but I changed my mind and decided to go to Hawaii.

"Anyway," Alan Krisp continued, "at about noon, I drove over to Bob's house. He usually comes home for lunch at about that time, and I wanted to discuss my hotel reservations with him. You see, Bob is a travel agent as well as an old friend, and I booked my trip through him."

Frank and Joe looked at each other, embarrassed by their long string of mistakes. Alan Krisp and Robert Blane didn't appear to be the saboteurs. But if they had nothing to do with the case, then why had they been knocked out?

"Let's get back to what happened here," said Frank. "You didn't see who hit you?"

Alan Krisp got to his feet slowly, helped by Frank and Joe. "Well, after we went over the details of my trip, Bob invited me to stay for lunch," Krisp said, trying to remember. "We took our sandwiches into the living room and Bob turned on the radio. Then we sat down to eat. Before I knew it, I felt a conk on the head and that was it—until now."

"The back door lock was tampered with," said Joe. Then he asked, "You didn't hear anything?"

"Not a thing," Krisp replied. "I guess the sound of the radio covered any sound the intruder made."

Blane was conscious and on his feet by this time, but his memory was the same as Krisp's. His friend had been sitting off to the side and behind him, and he had been unaware that Krisp had been hit on the head.

"Has anything been stolen?" asked Frank. He wondered if the attack was part of a robbery and had nothing to do with the sabotage at the CompuCar factory.

"I've still got my wallet," said Blane.

"Me, too," echoed Krisp. "And I'm carrying a lot of cash."

"Then it wasn't robbery," Frank said with finality. "But why would anyone want to knock you out?"

The two men looked down at the floor. It

seemed to Frank and Joe that neither man was willing to offer a name. They seemed very reluctant to answer that question.

Frank and Joe didn't know what to make of that. They needed a chance to think, to put all the pieces together. They weren't going to get that chance.

Just then, Chief Collig and Con Riley rushed into the house through the open front door.

"What happened here?" Collig demanded. "We picked up the ambulance's radio call back at the station. It said that Joe Hardy had reported two unconscious men at this address. We got here as fast as we could."

Frank quickly filled them in. When he was finished, the chief pointed toward the kitchen and said, "Follow me."

Wondering what Collig had in mind, they trailed after him, leaving Krisp and Blane behind in the living room.

In a low voice, Collig said, "It looks like this case is all wrapped up."

"What do you mean?" asked Joe, surprised.

"I have to admit I didn't think Blane was in on this, but I guess he was," Collig began. "Anyway, it seems to me that Arnold Stockard must have figured out that Krisp and his friend were out to destroy the CompuCar Company. And once he knew that, he came over here and took his own revenge. In the process, he made it clear to his two enemies that they'd get worse if they tried anything in the future."

"It sounds like you know something we don't know," Frank said softly.

Chief Collig smiled. "Good guess," he said approvingly. "After checking out Krisp in the files, we took a look at everyone else connected to the case and came across an interesting tidbit. Get this: Arnold Stockard had union troubles two years ago. Know what he did?"

Frank and Joe both shook their heads.

"Stockard had a secret meeting with the union boss and hit him over the head. Knocked him out!" said Collig, emphasizing the point by slamming his hand against the kitchen table. "The union settled the very next day. Sounds like we have a pattern here, huh?"

"It's possible," admitted Frank, "but that means that Krisp and Blane are the saboteurs, and I'm not so sure I believe that anymore."

"Same goes for me," Joe put in.

"You're forgetting something," said Collig. "Motive. There's no reason that I can

87

think of why these two guys should get knocked out unless it's to send them a message.

"Now, I may not have any proof to back up what I'm saying," continued Collig, "but I've been a cop a long time. I know that history can tell you a whole lot more than a single eyewitness account. If Stockard used some muscle to get what he wanted once, he probably did it again. And I'll tell you this," he added, "if the sabotage stops, then I was right—Krisp and Blane were the saboteurs."

"I can't figure it out," said Frank, as they cruised toward their home across town, Joe at the wheel. "Why would Stockard hire us in the first place if he already knew that Krisp and Blane were to blame for all the sabotage?"

Neither of them had an answer for that. Collig had to be wrong. But where was the key to the puzzle?

The CC-2000 glided smoothly down the road. For the time being, it was behaving itself. Frank sat back and closed his eyes. He stayed like that for a while, silent and unmoving, until he suddenly sat up straight and said, "Chief Collig is right about one thing: we've got to focus on the motive. If we think Krisp and Blane aren't the saboteurs, then we need to figure out *why* they were knocked out."

"Maybe they know who the real saboteur is but aren't telling," suggested Joe. "It could be the saboteur hit them as a warning, you know, to keep them from talking. You saw how they clammed up when we asked them who might have clunked them."

"Yeah. It's a thought, but I don't know. I got the feeling they know something that they aren't telling, but not because they're scared. It's more because they aren't sure."

Joe glanced down at the car's dashboard and laughed. "Maybe we should ask the car to tell us why the saboteur hit those two guys."

"This car couldn't do any worse than *we're* doing," Frank said glumly. "But it sounds as if you're convinced the saboteur is the same person who hit Krisp and Blane."

"Yeah, I guess I am. And if that's true—" Joe suddenly slammed on the brakes and grabbed his brother by the arm. "That's it!" he blurted out with a flash of understanding.

"What?"

"I know why Krisp and Blane were knocked out! It makes perfect sense."

"Don't keep it a secret. What is it?"

"Don't you see? They've been our prime

suspects," Joe explained, "but whoever the saboteur really is, he's obviously been arranging accidents at the factory around the times that either Krisp or Blane—or both of them—had no ready alibis."

"Right," said Frank, catching on. "The saboteur knew who the suspects were because he's been setting them up."

"You got it."

Frank's expression turned deadly serious. "If you're right about this," he said, "then Krisp and Blane were put out of commission so that they could be blamed for something that's going to happen tonight at the factory. After still more sabotage, who would believe their excuse that they had been knocked out?"

"Nobody," said Joe. "It might be hard to prove they were guilty, but the real culprit would have plenty of time to cover his trail." Joe glanced at his brother. "You know, we're the only ones who know that the saboteur is going to strike again tonight."

"That's right," said Frank. "And that means that right now we're the only ones with a chance of catching him!"

10 Driven Crazy

"We'd better call Mr. Stockard and tell him the situation," said Frank.

"Good idea."

But then both of them groaned. They realized that the car phone was still broken.

"There's a gas station down this road," said Frank. "If I remember right, there's a phone booth in front of it."

They drove swiftly through the quiet streets, straining their eyes for the gas station.

"There! On the right!" cried Frank, pointing.

"I see it," said Joe, slowing down and pulling into the station.

"Do you have Stockard's number?" asked Joe as the car settled to a stop in front of the phone booth.

"It's right here," Frank replied, waving a business card in his hand. He unbuckled his seat belt, climbed out of the car, and rushed to the phone.

It was out of order.

"Just our luck," said Frank, slamming the car door shut behind him. "Keep going."

They drove from one residential area to another without any luck.

"We're getting pretty close to our house," noted Joe. "If we don't find a phone soon, we might as well go slightly out of our way and call from home."

But just as he said that, they came across the Bayport Diner.

"We should have remembered this place," said Joe. "I mean, we spend enough time here with Iola and Callie. And right now, I could really use a piece of their excellent banana cream pie."

"Let's just hope they've got an excellent telephone—that works."

They pulled into the parking lot, and this time, both of them jumped out of the car and raced into the diner. They were lucky that no one else was using the telephone. Joe dug some change out of his pocket and handed it over to Frank, who dropped it into the machine and dialed.

Frank made a face and hung up.

"What is it?" asked Joe. "What's wrong?"

"Busy signal."

"This is an emergency," said Joe. "Call the operator and tell her to break into Stockard's conversation. We've got to get through."

Frank did as his brother suggested. But the operator reported back that the number they were trying to reach was a car phone and it appeared to be out of order. There was nothing she could do.

"Figures," said Joe, frustrated. "Maybe all these CompuCars are lemons."

"That wouldn't surprise me," Frank said absently. "Stockard would probably be better off collecting on the insurance than trying to sell a fleet of these expensive junkmobiles."

"Now, there's an interesting thought," said Joe.

"What is?"

"What you just said."

"What did I say?"

"That maybe the saboteur *is* Arnold Stockard. Maybe he's destroying his own company for the insurance money."

"Wait a minute," Frank said. "Stockard would have to be incredibly stupid to hire us—to hire anyone—to find himself."

"Think it through," Joe insisted. "We'd

be reporting everything we learn to Stockard, so it would be easy for him to keep one step ahead of us."

"I see what you mean, but you're forgetting something important," explained Frank. "Stockard dropped us off at his showroom and drove away. The steel beam that almost killed us fell after he had gone."

"He could have hired somebody to do that," Joe countered.

"Sure, but how could he have arranged it? Remember, he didn't plan on hiring us. It was Dad he had come out to see, and Stockard didn't know that Dad was out of town. And even when he hired us and gave us the CC-2000 to use, it was only because our van wasn't working—and he couldn't have known that."

"I'm way ahead of you," said Joe, nodding his head in reluctant agreement. "We were with Stockard the whole time after he hired us, and he never could have arranged for that steel beam to be dropped on our heads. Unless," he said softly, "that steel beam wasn't meant for us at all. Maybe it was Stockard that the saboteur was after.

"Think about it," Joe continued. "There were people at the showroom who knew Stockard was coming. Remember, he called ahead to the manager. Nobody knew, though, that he wasn't getting out of the car with us. Let's face it, somebody might have wanted to kill him so bad that they were willing to wipe us out at the same time."

"Hmmm," was all that Frank said. He was thinking about Dennis Belfree, the man who had been fired by Stockard.

But before Frank could say anything, Joe said, "We're wasting time. We still don't know who we're after. But we know he's going to strike again tonight."

As they hurried out of the diner, Joe glanced back over his shoulder at a banana cream pie in the display case. It looked delicious. There was no doubt about it—being a detective definitely had its drawbacks.

The sun had almost set by the time they left the diner. As soon as they were back in the car, Joe started up the CC-2000 and asked the car's computer to flip on the headlights. Then he backed out of their parking space. "We're going to be pretty embarrassed if the saboteur doesn't surface tonight," he said when they hit the street.

"If the saboteur doesn't show," Frank said grimly, "then we ought to give up being detectives."

Joe knew exactly what he meant. The saboteur had been ahead of them every step of the way. It was getting downright humiliating.

They drove toward the CompuCar factory, passing near their own neighborhood, when Frank happened to glance at the speedometer. "Hey, I know we're in a hurry, but you're going over the speed limit, Joe. Better watch it. We don't want to get stopped by a traffic cop."

When he looked down at the speedometer, Joe was surprised to find they were going faster than thirty-five miles per hour. He hadn't been pressing down very hard on the gas pedal. Just the same, he eased up slightly, expecting the car to slow down.

It didn't. In fact, the CC-2000 continued to pick up speed.

From forty miles per hour, the car inched up to forty-five. Joe took his foot off the gas pedal entirely. The car went even faster.

"What are you doing?" demanded Frank, realizing that they were now way over the speed limit.

"Nothing!" cried Joe. "I think the gas pedal is stuck." He yelled in frustration, "I can't believe it! First the electrical system, now the machinery!"

"Hit the brakes!" shouted Frank.

Joe did just that, but the car leapt forward like a shot. Joe couldn't believe it, so he hit the brake again—and the car jumped forward once more, causing both Frank and Joe's heads to snap back against the headrests.

The brake was acting just like the gas pedal.

By now, the CC-2000 was careening down the streets of Bayport at seventy miles an hour. It was going faster and faster—and Joe had no idea how to stop it!

11 CompuCrash!

Frank and Joe were lucky that it was after rush hour. The streets were relatively empty of cars, but not completely empty.

They were speeding toward the back end of a truck. It was almost as if the eighteen-wheeler in front of them was hardly moving.

"Order the car to put on the brakes!" shouted Frank over the screaming engine.

Joe hit the button on the steering wheel and yelled, "Stop!"

Nothing happened.

"Stop!" Joe repeated.

"Does not compute," answered the electronic voice of the CC-2000.

The car zoomed closer to the much-slower-moving truck. They were just seconds away from slamming into it!

The road had just two lanes. There was a guardrail on their right. With the truck in front of them, Joe couldn't see if there was

98

any traffic coming toward them from the other direction.

Joe had no other choice. He turned the wheel to his left and entered the other lane. He was beginning to pass the truck when he saw the lights of an oncoming car. He had to pass the truck and get back in the right lane before it was too late.

Speed wasn't a problem. The CC-2000 was now going eighty miles an hour. But controlling the car *was* a definite problem. Getting it to sharply change lanes had the rear wheels fishtailing. They passed the truck in two seconds flat. But when Joe steered back into the right lane, the back end of the CC-2000 swung all the way over to the right and bashed against the guard-rail!

For one terrible moment the car was zig-zagging wildly down the road at eighty-five miles per hour. But Joe hung in there, wrestling the wheel under control.

Both Frank and Joe let the air out of their lungs. But they quickly held their breath again because up ahead was a traffic light. They were nearing a busy intersection and the light was red! Joe looked at the speedometer. Ninety miles per hour. At that speed it was becoming difficult to keep the car under control even while going in a straight line.

"I've got to hold on to the wheel," cried Joe. "It's up to you," he told his brother, "to find a way to stop this thing!"

Frank understood. He immediately began punching buttons on the dashboard and fiddling with every gadget he could get his hands on, hoping to find a new connection to the brakes.

He turned the radio from FM to AM.

He turned the heater on.

He tried the air conditioning.

None of it worked. The car was up to ninety-five miles per hour. Cars zipped through the green light at the busy street ahead. Frank and Joe were hurtling toward the intersection like a bullet.

Joe leaned on the horn. But that didn't work either. Instead of blaring out a warning, water sprayed up onto the windshield, making it nearly impossible for Joe to see where they were going. All he could do was keep the steering wheel steady and try to go straight.

Even though they couldn't see anything, the other cars could see them. A car already in the intersection was nearly broadsided by the CC-2000, but the driver swerved out of the way at the last second. A car entering the intersection from the other direction also swerved out of the way, nearly hitting the first car.

The sound of tires squealing and horns blaring filled the air. Frank and Joe blazed through the intersection so fast, though, that they didn't hear a thing!

But the worst was yet to come. The street, which so far had been straight, began to wind and twist and turn. Now, at one hundred miles per hour, the CC-2000 was on the verge of literally flying off the road!

Frank kept up his efforts to find the brakes.

He moved his seat forward, then back. He punched the button that was supposed to turn on the emergency flashers.

Again, nothing worked.

Meanwhile, Joe struggled to keep the car on the road. When the street hooked to the left, Joe shouted, "Hold on!" The CC-2000 took the turn on two wheels, nearly flipping over. Finally, the car fell back down on all four tires with a hard thump. Frank and Joe hit their heads on the roof, but Joe clung fiercely to the steering wheel.

But before they reached another turn, they had to somehow survive a steep hill. Climbing the hill wasn't the problem. In fact, the CC-2000 revved up to one hundred

101

and ten miles per hour going straight uphill. The problem was that after they topped the crest of the hill, the road dropped right out from underneath them.

They were airborne!

It was as if they were on water skis and had just made a spectacular jump off a ramp.

The car soared over the road below until the front of the CC-2000 nosed downward and began to fall. It was like a wild ride in an amusement park. But they might have to pay for this ride with their lives.

The car hit the roadway with a bone-jarring crash. And it wasn't only their bones that were jarred. The undercarriage of the CC-2000 took a terrible beating, smashing against the pavement. Miraculously, the tires didn't blow, but the wheels were bent. The car was incapable of going in a straight line, but it still wouldn't stop. Now they were screaming down the road at an incredible one hundred and twenty—and they were all over the roadway!

The car's headlights flashed on a sign. The sign flew past them on a curve so fast that Joe didn't see it. But Frank did. It said, "Dead End Ahead."

Frank redoubled his already frantic efforts to find the brakes. But there wasn't much more that he could do. He had already hit just about every button and gadget on the car. There were just a few things left that he hadn't tried yet.

As much as he hated to do it, he unfastened his seat belt. The car didn't slow down. Then he tried opening the car door a crack, but that didn't work either.

Finally, unable to think of anything else, he reached across his brother's body and turned off the car's headlights.

"No!" shouted Joe. The road disappeared into blackness.

But the brakes suddenly kicked in, gripping the street! The tires screeched and burned on the pavement. The smell of burning rubber filled their nostrils. They were sure it was the last thing they'd ever smell.

The brakes locked and the car began to spin. They felt as if the car was going to flip over onto its right side. But then the right front tire exploded from the pressure, shooting the vehicle back up to the left so it didn't tip over. Then the left front tire blew up. The car skidded forward on the front axle at sixty, fifty, forty miles an hour.

They were slowing down.

Thirty-five miles per hour . . . thirty . . . twenty-five . . .

Then they crashed through what felt like a barrier, leaving the road. They bumped along at twenty miles per hour . . . fifteen . . . ten . . . five . . . and then they finally rolled to a stop.

Frank and Joe leapt out of the car. They didn't want to spend another second in that motorized deathtrap. But when their eyes became accustomed to the darkness and they saw where they had stopped, Frank and Joe realized just how lucky they really were. The car had rolled to within five yards of a cliff overlooking a lake. Had they gone much farther, they would have hurtled down to their deaths in the water below.

Frank and Joe collapsed onto the grass, shaken and exhausted. They lay under the stars, next to the car, until they both stopped trembling. Finally, Frank propped himself up on his elbows and said, "How could Arnold Stockard sell a car like that?"

"How could he even give it away?" Joe joked weakly.

Frank stared at the battered hulk that hissed and steamed next to them in the grass. "At first the computerized stuff the car did was kind of neat—even the mess-ups were funny. And they certainly weren't threatening. But I never thought this would happen."

"You know," said Joe thoughtfully, "maybe we ought to take a look at the

CC-2000's computer disk. I'd sure like to know why the computer couldn't stop the car."

"I'd like to know that myself," agreed Frank. "But we've got to get to the CompuCar factory."

"Yeah, but how?" said Joe, gesturing toward the wreck beside them.

"You've got a good point," said Frank.

"Hey," said Joe, brightening, "we're not that far from home. If I've got my bearings, we're only three or four miles away. If we jog at a fast pace, we ought to get there in less than half an hour. Then we can borrow Mom's car and race over to the factory."

"Good thinking," said Frank. "And as long as we'll be home," he added, "let's do what you suggested and stick the car's computer disk into our own P.C. and check it out. I just hope it's compatible."

They quickly located the car's computer and removed the CompuCar program disk. Then they took off for home at a hard, steady run.

With sweat dripping off their faces, Frank and Joe stormed through the front door and ran up the stairs.

"Frank? Joe? Is that you?" their mother called out from the living room.

From the top of the landing, Frank replied, "Yes, it's us, Mom."

Laura Hardy stepped into the hallway, looked up at her sons, and said, "I didn't hear you drive up. What happened to your fancy car?"

Frank and Joe exchanged glances. They didn't want to frighten their mother, so Joe simply offered, "We had to hoof it back home. The car broke down."

"Nothing serious, I hope," she said. "It was awfully nice of Mr. Stockard to loan you a car. I wouldn't want to think you didn't take proper care of it."

"It wasn't our fault, Mom," replied Frank. "In fact, we brought home the floppy disk from the car's computer to see if we can figure out what went wrong."

"Well, if you need me, I'll be in the living room," she said.

Before she left the hallway, though, Frank asked if they could borrow her car.

"The keys are on the kitchen table," she said. "By the way, your father said he might be home later tonight. He called while you were out. He asked how your case was progressing and wished you luck."

"A little luck wouldn't hurt," said Joe.

"As long as it isn't bad luck," amended Frank. "We've had enough of that already."

Laura Hardy smiled indulgently and then left her sons to their work. They raced to the computer in Frank's room, booting it up. Then they slid the CompuCar program disk into the machine.

Frank's fingers flitted over the keyboard, giving the computer specific commands to check the CompuCar disk. At first, nothing seemed to be wrong with the car's computer program; it showed everything as normal.

"Keep trying," urged Joe. "Whatever that computer disk is, we know it isn't normal."

"That's the interesting thing," said Frank thoughtfully. "It's as if the disk has been coded to keep anyone from finding the problem. Why would somebody do—"

Frank stopped. His mouth fell open as the screen suddenly lit up with a whole string of malfunctions.

"Now we're cooking!" said Joe.

"More than cooking," Frank added, pointing to the top line on the screen. "Frying is more like it. Maybe even burning up. Look at that!"

Joe squinted at the information on the screen, then shrugged. "I don't understand. It says that the malfunctions it's listing aren't really malfunctions at all. What does that mean?"

"It means," explained Frank, "that the

107

malfunctions were programmed into the disk. In other words, the CompuCar floppy was purposefully programmed with a built-in glitch. It automatically made the on-board computer slowly break down with use. That's why our CC-2000 started acting more and more bizarre. I've read about stuff like this. The experts call it a computer virus."

Joe sat down on the edge of the bed and let everything Frank had said seep into his brain. After a short while he stared back at the computer screen and slowly said, "Destroying the computer of the CompuCar is the ultimate sabotage for a car like this."

"And there's only one man capable of doing it," Frank said boldly.

12 Before It's Too Late

"Edward Hartman is the man we're after," said Frank. "There's no doubt about it. He's the only one with the computer know-how who could have sabotaged this program."

Joe didn't disagree. He had reached the same conclusion. And finally all the nagging questions, all the pieces of the puzzle, began to fall into place. "Remember that phone call warning we got in the car?" said Joe with a sudden realization.

"What about it?"

"There was this rush of air on the line before the guy said anything. I didn't know what it was then, but now I think I do. Hartman took some vitamin C at the factory and said he was fighting off a cold. I think that sound on the phone was him sneezing. But wait a minute," he said, suddenly unsure. "What about Alan Krisp? Why was he spying on us when Hartman was giving us the tour of the factory?"

"He wasn't," replied Frank. "He was spying on Hartman! Chances are he suspected him but had no proof. I bet that's why he wouldn't say anything earlier when we asked him who he thought had hit him. Blane probably suspected him, too."

"All right, I can see that," said Joe. "Yeah. And I can definitely see that Hartman built that bomb. Remember what Con Riley said? That it was the most sophisticated time bomb he had ever seen? Only a brilliant scientist could have built something that complicated. But what about the steel beam?" asked Joe, checking out their theory. "How could he have dropped it on us?"

"Simple. If we assume that he was the one who bugged Stockard's car—which would have been easy for a guy like that—then he could have sped over to the showroom building ahead of us."

"It's possible," agreed Joe.

"And I'd be willing to bet that he borrowed a black car with heavily tinted windows from the factory lot," Frank continued. "Because if he really was the one who dropped that beam on us, once he failed, he had to beat us back to the factory."

"Yeah. Maybe trying to kill us again along the way," said Joe, remembering.

"That car that tried to run us off the road," Frank pointed out, "was heading in the same direction we were. Hartman probably felt that even if he didn't kill us, he had to at least stall us from reaching the factory ahead of him. It wouldn't have looked good for him if he wasn't there when we arrived."

"Hartman's our saboteur, all right," Joe said, "but what we still don't know is *why*. What's his motive? Why is he trying to drive the CompuCar Company out of business? It's his genius that makes these cars work in the first place. Isn't his own reputation going to be ruined if the CompuCar Company is a flop?"

"Maybe he doesn't care about that," suggested Frank. "Remember how he said that there were a lot of people who were taken advantage of by Arnold Stockard?"

"Yes."

"Maybe Hartman was one of them. Maybe our scientist is after revenge—at any cost."

"It's time we stopped talking theory and started taking action," said Joe, jumping to his feet. "We've got to find out what Hartman is up to and stop him—before it's too late."

"I just hope it isn't too late already," said

Frank, as they scrambled out of his bedroom and down to the kitchen to pick up their mother's car keys.

They were at the door, ready to dash out, when Frank said, "Wait a minute. We'd better call Chief Collig and tell him to meet us at the CompuCar factory."

Joe smiled. "He thinks this case is all wrapped up. Boy, is he in for a surprise."

Frank dialed the Bayport police station number, but the chief had gone home for the night. "Is Con Riley there?" he asked.

"Just one minute."

A moment later Frank heard a phone ring.

"Detective Riley, here," said the strong, familiar voice on the other end of the line.

Frank quickly filled their friend in on their discovery. When he finished there was dead silence.

"Are you still there?" Frank asked.

"I'm here. I'm just trying to figure out how I'm going to reach the chief. He was going to the movies with his wife. But don't worry. I'll get him."

"We're going to the factory," said Frank. "Can you and the chief meet us there?"

"We'll be there as soon as we can," promised Riley. "In the meantime, be careful.

This Hartman is obviously a very—I repeat —*very* dangerous man."

Their mother's car was an old but sturdy station wagon. It squeaked and rattled as if it was on the verge of falling apart, the radio didn't work, and the odometer had broken several years ago. But at least it worked. It felt great to Frank and Joe to be in control of a car again.

"Tell the car to go faster," Joe kidded as they rumbled along the road to the CompuCar factory.

Frank pretended to push an imaginary button on the steering wheel. "Come on, you wonderful old piece of junk. Put on some speed!"

The car surprised them by responding with a loud backfire.

Frank and Joe laughed about that for half a mile.

After they had been driving for ten minutes, they left the residential area of Bayport and entered the industrial park at the city's outskirts. The CompuCar factory was straight ahead. They could see its gently lit outlines farther down the road. Then, all of a sudden, the CompuCar building was lit up from the inside out with a blinding flash of light.

For one split second every window in the factory shone as bright as the beacon of a lighthouse. Then the lights just as quickly dimmed to their normal level.

"Strange. Very strange," said Joe.

"It looked like some kind of power surge," Frank noted.

"I've got a sneaking suspicion that Edward Hartman had something to do with that."

Frank parked, turned the car engine off, and then the two of them headed for the factory's front door.

Frank looked around the parking lot. "Chief Collig and Con Riley aren't here yet," he said.

"If the chief doesn't believe us about the computer virus, he may not come at all," Joe said softly. "We'd better be ready to handle Hartman all by ourselves."

"Then let's go do it," said Frank.

Joe nodded and swung open the factory's heavy, soundproof front door. But as soon as they stepped inside the building, they heard screams of panic. Then a huge crowd of people came running down the hall right at them!

13 Factory Frenzy

Frank was pushed out of the way, but Joe wasn't so lucky. He was knocked to the ground as countless numbers of terrified CompuCar employees ran out of the building. Some of them saw Joe and tried to jump over him. But most didn't look and didn't care. They trampled over him, their feet pounding down on his back.

Joe curled up in a ball and covered his head, waiting for the stampede to slow down long enough for him to roll out of the way. When the worst was finally over, Frank rushed over to his brother. "Are you all right?" he asked anxiously.

Joe lifted his head. "Bruised, but I'll be okay. Just help me up."

Joe was wobbly, but he managed to shake off most of his aches and pains and said, "Those people were pretty spooked. We'd better find out what's going on in there."

They hurried along an empty corridor in the main-floor office area. The assembly lines were up ahead. Frank and Joe could hear the machines and robots at work. If the assembly line was still going, why had the people run away?

They found the answer when the corridor opened up and they saw what had happened. The computer-controlled assembly line robots had gone totally berserk!

One robot, used to pick up fenders and then bolt them onto car chassis, was picking up and throwing fenders in every direction. Another robot was ripping the doors off car bodies, while yet another one rhythmically crashed down on the middle of the assembly line, smashing windshields, and denting hoods, roofs, and trunks.

It was the same everywhere they looked. The robots were turning the factory into a car junkyard!

"We've got to find Hartman," said Frank. "He's the cause of all this."

"I bet he's around here somewhere, enjoying the destruction," Joe replied bitterly.

They set out across the factory floor, searching for Hartman. But it wasn't easy. Not by a long shot. A flying headlight came soaring down at Frank's head at a sharp angle. He ducked, and it barely missed him.

116

An instant later, there was a crash and a cry of pain. The headlight hit Joe in the shoulder. Luckily, the heavy glass didn't shatter, but the force of the impact sent Joe reeling off his feet.

Frank pulled his brother to his feet. "Can you go on?" he asked.

Joe was about to answer yes, but before he could say a word, he spotted somebody across the factory floor. It was a man, who had either been struck by something or had ducked out of sight. Hartman?

"Over there!" Joe pointed. "Let's go!"

"You sure you're up to it?" persisted Frank.

Instead of answering, Joe took off at top speed across the floor. He dodged windshield wipers that flew like knives and metal air filters that sailed in every direction like deadly Frisbees.

Frank was right behind him.

They were getting close to where Joe had seen the man disappear when they heard someone cry out, "Help! Somebody, please help me!"

Frank and Joe ran toward the sound. After narrowly avoiding getting slugged by a robot whose arms were swinging out uselessly over the narrow aisle, all they found was a huge pile of tires. Another robot was tossing them

117

onto an ever-growing mountain of rubber. But then they heard the call for help again.

"It's coming from underneath the tires!" shouted Frank. "Somebody is being buried alive down there!"

Frank and Joe worked furiously. They were in a race to throw the tires off the man faster than the robot could keep piling them on. In the beginning, they were winning. But humans get tired, robots don't. The Hardys started to slow down.

"Hurry! Please! I can't breathe!" cried the man under the tires.

"This isn't working," wheezed Frank. "We've got to try something else."

"If we can knock over that whole pile of tires in one shot," suggested Joe, "we'll get that guy out in no time."

"But how are we going to do that?"

"With a little help from a friend," said Joe with a smile. "I've got an idea." He picked up one of the fenders that had been tossed nearby and jammed one end of it into the mechanical paws of the robot that had earlier almost decked them. The robot swung the fender around in its relentless mechanical motion, slamming it against the side of the rubber mountain. A few tires at the top began to tumble over.

The robot hit the pile over and over again.

It wasn't long before the tires began to shower down the far side of the rubber mountain like an avalanche.

They could see the man struggling under the remaining tires. Frank and Joe bent down underneath the constantly swinging fender and pulled the man to safety.

It was Arnold Stockard!

The president of the CompuCar Company was dazed and disoriented. He swayed on his feet as if he were on a ship in a stormy sea. "My factory," he kept wailing. "Look what's happening to my factory."

"We're going to try and save it," Frank said. "We know what's wrong—it's a computer virus."

"A computer virus?"

"There's no time to explain it now," Frank said hurriedly. "Have you seen Edward Hartman? We've got to find him!"

"Edward? Yes. But he's already taking care of the problem," said Stockard.

"Taking care of the problem? No way!" said Joe. "He *is* the problem."

"What?" Stockard said, disbelief etched on his face.

"Just tell us where he is," pleaded Frank.

"I . . . I . . . gave him the combination to the safe that's upstairs in my office," said Stockard anxiously. "He said he needed to . . . to adjust the main computer programs."

"Sabotage them is more like it," said Joe.

Frank and Joe left Stockard and edged their way to the factory wall where there were no robots running amok. Then they ran toward the elevators. One of the elevator doors was open, so the Hardys piled inside and punched the button for the seventh floor.

Big mistake.

The computer virus had spread to the rest of the factory's computer-operated machinery, and the elevator shot up toward the roof of the building like a rocket. The door never opened at the seventh floor. In fact, it looked as if the door was never going to open. It didn't matter what buttons Frank and Joe hit on the control panel. The elevator ignored them all.

"We're going to crash into the top of the shaft!" Frank warned. "Get down on the floor and brace yourself!"

They both dove face down to the elevator's floor. A second later, Frank's words proved true. The elevator smashed against the roof. The Hardys were thrown around the inside of the elevator like a pair of dice rattling around the inside of a cup.

They were waiting for the inevitable descent back to the bottom. But the elevator didn't fall. It was stuck, its cables snarled in the hoist mechanism.

"We've got to get out of here before this elevator decides to return to earth," said Joe. He looked up and pointed to a spot just above Frank's head. "There's a trap door up there."

Frank didn't say anything. He simply climbed up onto the elevator's inside railing, steadied himself, and then pushed open the trap door. He climbed onto the roof of the elevator and then reached down to help Joe up through the opening.

They were in luck. There was a ladder built into the side of the elevator shaft.

"I guess they put ladders up here for times when the elevator is busted, so repairmen can move up and down the shaft," said Joe.

"That's great for the repairmen," Frank answered. "They get to grab right onto the ladder from whatever floor they're on. We've got to jump toward it from all the way out here in the middle of the shaft."

"Scared?" asked Joe.

"You bet. Aren't you?"

"Yeah. I was just checking. I'd hate to be the only one."

"I'll jump first," Frank offered. But it

wasn't Joe's way to stand by and wait patiently for his part of the action. Just before Frank leapt across the space between the elevator car and the ladder on the wall, Joe suddenly shouted, "Here goes!" and vaulted across the opening.

He didn't calculate the angle very well. His right hand missed the ladder completely. So did his right foot. But with a desperate lunge, his left hand grabbed hold of one of the ladder's bars, and his left foot found a rung. He dangled there precariously until he managed to swing his right hand over onto one of the ladder's rungs. Finally, he swung his right foot over and planted it onto a rung.

Joe was safe.

"I'm going to start climbing down till I find a way out. Just don't jump and fall on top of me, okay?" Joe said with forced humor.

After Joe had climbed down a full floor, Frank took the plunge. He jumped and hit the ladder right in the center!

"Made it," he called to his brother.

"I knew you could do it!" Joe called back.

They both climbed down the shaft until Joe found a pair of elevator doors that were constantly opening and closing. He timed his jump and flew between the open doors, rolling onto the carpeted hallway. Less than thirty seconds later Frank sailed through those doors, too.

"What floor are we on?" asked Frank.

Joe had already checked. "Eighth floor," he said. "All the doors are numbered in the eight hundreds."

"Then Hartman is just one floor below."

They raced to the stairwell, taking the steps two at a time. They knew that if the scientist got his hands on CompuCar's main computer programs, he'd ruin them the way he ruined all the other disks. They had to stop Hartman from getting those disks and programming them with the computer virus. And they had to stop him now!

Frank and Joe exploded through the seventh-floor stairwell doors at top speed. All the doors along the corridors were closed. All, that is, except one. The door to Stockard's office was wide open.

They ran toward the open door and into Stockard's office. Hartman was standing behind Stockard's desk. The safe on the wall behind him was open. In one of Hartman's hands was a small box that he had obviously taken from the safe.

In the other hand was a pistol—and it was aimed directly at Frank and Joe!

14 No Escape

Had they entered the room more cautiously, Frank and Joe might have stopped and put their hands up. But they had so much momentum from their race down the hallway that they couldn't have stopped even if they had wanted to. Instead, the instant they saw the gun, they both dove head first onto the floor, without missing a beat.

"Get up," ordered Hartman, rounding the desk.

Frank and Joe ignored Hartman's command. Instead, they scrambled behind a sofa. Hartman gave a short laugh as he continued around the desk. Frank and Joe heard him close the door to the office and move back to the desk, sitting down in Arnold Stockard's chair.

"Now, let's be reasonable," Hartman said calmly. "It's a bit ridiculous for you two to be hiding behind that sofa, wouldn't you agree? Just come out with your hands up and you won't get hurt." He added more menacingly, "Remember, I have the gun."

Frank and Joe looked at each other. Their retreat behind the sofa had gained them some time, as they had hoped. But now they had to go into action. Somehow, they had to reach Hartman and get the gun away from him.

Frank gestured for Joe to circle around Stockard's desk to the right. He was going to circle to the left. Hartman could look in only one direction at a time. It was their only hope.

"You can't escape me!" yelled Hartman. He stood up and aimed the gun at the chair behind which Frank had been hiding. But Frank was already gone.

Hartman knew what the Hardys were planning. It was easy enough to guess. They had split up and were trying to surround him. He smiled.

"I've got your brother covered!" he exclaimed. "Come out with your hands up or I'll shoot him."

Frank and Joe were hidden from each other's view. They both thought that Hartman had captured the other. Hoping to

125

save each other's lives, both brothers surrendered.

When they stood up, Hartman swung his gun around to cover them. The computer genius laughed. "Funny, isn't it," he said, "that a lie can sometimes become the truth. Now I've got you both covered." Then the smile disappeared from his lips and he growled, "I don't know how you two found me out, but you're going to be sorry you did. *Very* sorry."

"Listen, Mr. Hartman," Frank said, trying to keep his voice calm, "we figure you must have a grudge against Arnold Stockard. But if you destroy the CompuCar Company, thousands of people are going to be thrown out of work. Lives are going to be wrecked. Is that what you want?"

"I don't care about any of that," Hartman sneered. "Some people will lose their jobs. So what? People lose jobs all the time. They'll find other jobs. But Arnold Stockard will be totally, thoroughly, and completely ruined. *That's* what I care about."

"What did he do that was so terrible?" asked Frank, stalling for time. He hoped to keep Hartman talking until Chief Collig and Con Riley showed up. *If* they showed up.

"Stockard did the worst thing he could have ever done to me," Hartman replied.

"He shackled my genius and then he stole my creation."

"What do you mean?" asked Joe, joining in on his brother's stalling campaign.

"Stockard hired me to create a new kind of computer-operated automobile," Hartman explained, his eyes growing wild with the memory. "Everyone said it was impossible, that the technology just wasn't advanced enough. But I slaved at it day and night. For months. For years. And against all odds, I finally did it!" For a brief moment, Hartman beamed with satisfaction. "It was a major breakthrough, a leap into the future," he went on grandly.

Suddenly Hartman's eyes grew dark. "Oh, Stockard gave me the credit for it. He even gave me a promotion," he said harshly. "But since I was only an employee when I invented the CompuCar, the patent belongs to the company. Stockard promised that I'd get a share of the profits. Instead," Hartman roared, his face turning red with anger, "when the money started rolling in, he kept it all!

"I swore I'd get even with him," Hartman said coldly, "but I played it cagey. Just like Stockard himself. I pretended to be pleased that he gave me the credit while he took the money. And I pretended to be satisfied with the paltry salary he paid me while he made a fortune!

"I smiled, I was friendly, I was the best employee he ever had," Hartman continued. "But I was plotting against him at every turn. And I was doing it in a way that no one would ever discover until after it was too late. I was using the very same computers that I had created to destroy what my genius had built. And tonight I'll have my final revenge."

"But you've already programmed the computer virus into the CompuCars and the factory machinery. Isn't that enough?" demanded Frank.

"No!" Hartman cried in a shrill voice. "It's not enough. It'll never be enough. So far, I've only set out to destroy Stockard's machines. When I program my computer virus into the main computer disks," he said, shaking the small box in his hand, "then I'll have begun the destruction of all the CompuCar records, documents, and files that exist. They'll never in a million years be able to put this company back together again. They won't know who worked for them, how much they paid for materials, what their taxes were—nothing. Once the glitch works its way through the system, the numbers and letters will all be jumbled, and they'll never, ever be unscrambled."

"But the company computers are in constant touch with the computers in banks and other companies," said Joe, horrified at the implication of Hartman's plan. "The virus will spread through the phone lines and ultimately infect every computer in the world," he said. "You can't do this!"

"You think I care about any of that?" he shouted, waving his gun wildly.

While Hartman had been talking, Frank had been slowly edging his way toward one of the shade-covered windows behind Stockard's desk. Now he was close enough. He reached out a hand and quickly yanked the shade. It flew up with a loud snap. Joe jumped in surprise.

So did Hartman.

Joe took a chance and dove across the desk, hoping to disarm the gun-wielding maniac.

But Hartman was too quick for him. He stepped out of the way, leaving Joe sprawled over the desk, reaching for empty space. An instant later, Joe felt the warm barrel of the pistol's muzzle against the side of his head.

"That's enough of *that*," said Hartman. "Get back there with your brother."

Joe slid off the desk.

"Nice try," Frank whispered.

"Not nice enough," muttered Joe.

"It seems I've wasted more than enough time explaining my reasons to you," Hartman announced. "I suppose I was impressed with you for having realized that I was the saboteur. I thought I had really fooled you with that blackout I caused right in front of your eyes. I simply told the computer to turn off all the lights at a certain time, and you had no idea it was me. Or so I thought."

"No, you fooled us," admitted Frank. "And you might have kept right on fooling us except you were just a little too clever."

"Really?" Hartman asked with genuine interest. As a scientist, he wanted to know what he had done wrong.

"Tonight, when our CompuCar went bonkers, we discovered the computer virus," Frank slowly explained. "We realized that you were the only person who could have done it."

"Ah, yes," said Hartman. "I was sure that when your car reacted to the computer virus, it would have crashed and killed you both. But I didn't know when. My mistake was that I left it to chance. Well, now I'll know for the next time."

"There isn't going to be any next time," announced Joe.

"That's true. Not for you two, anyway."

"Not for you either," Joe continued. "Arnold Stockard knows about you. We saw him downstairs and told him you were the saboteur."

Hartman frowned. This was unexpected news.

Joe poured it on. "We also called the police before we came over here," he said, even though he had a feeling Collig and Riley weren't going to show up after all. There was no point in holding back anymore. Maybe they could use the police as a bluff.

"The police, you say?"

"That's right," said Joe. "So you might as well give up now before you get into any more serious trouble. The sabotage charge is bad enough. So is your clubbing of Alan Krisp and Robert Blane."

"So you know about that, too?" Hartman asked, raising an eyebrow.

"We know that and one other thing," said Joe. "That you're all finished. Put that gun away, give us the computer disks, and give yourself up."

"You must be joking." Hartman laughed. "Even if what you say is true—and I doubt that it is—I'd never give up. Let the police catch me. So what? All I want is my revenge. And I'm going to have it before they lock me up." Then he threw back his head and laughed even louder.

"What's so funny?" asked Joe.

"Isn't it obvious? If you actually told me the truth about the police, then you gave me a much needed warning that they're coming," he cackled. "So I'll play it safe and not dawdle. Come with me," he ordered, gesturing with the pistol in his hands. "I'm going to let you in on the end of the computer age."

At gunpoint, Frank and Joe walked ahead of Hartman toward the door.

"Where are we going?" asked Frank.

"We're going to the lab Stockard made me share with a chemist. I didn't even get my own office!" he said. "It's down the hall.

"Soon, you're going to watch me program a computer virus onto these master disks," he added, clutching the box close to his chest. "Then I'm going to put them in the company's main computer. Within seconds the virus will begin to spread and, when it does, it will be unstoppable."

They left the office and entered the hallway.

132

"Turn right," said Hartman.

There was nothing they could do except follow his orders.

"Around the corner," he commanded, as they passed the stairwell.

They were just rounding the bend when the sound of a police siren reached their ears.

Instinctively, all of them—including Hartman—stopped and listened. The computer genius seemed genuinely surprised. He had come to the same conclusion that Joe had—that the police really weren't coming. There was a window next to the stairwell and he turned his head in order to catch a glimpse of the police cars entering the parking lot below.

Hartman had given Frank and Joe an opening—and they took it.

Frank spun around and aimed a karate chop at Hartman's gun hand. At the force of the blow, the scientist lost his grip on the pistol and it clattered against the wall next to the window, then fell to the floor.

At the same time, Joe reached out and snatched the box of computer disks from Hartman's other hand.

Hartman was already reaching for the gun on the floor as Frank and Joe pushed through the stairwell doors. They knew he was going to be right behind them, but if they could race down those stairs fast enough, they just might get away.

It was going to be close.

"Stop or I'll shoot!" Hartman cried.

15 Trapped Again

Frank and Joe didn't stop at Hartman's warning. They knew he'd shoot at them, but they also knew that hitting a moving target wasn't that easy. Hartman was a computer genius, not a marksman.

They kept on running.

It seemed as if they were racing down the stairs in slow motion. Each second lasted an eternity. But their time was just about up; the sound of Hartman's gun being cocked echoed in the stairwell.

"We're almost there!" Frank shouted over his shoulder, urging his brother on. They were turning into the bend in the stairwell. Just a few more steps and they'd be out of Edward Hartman's gunsights.

But when Frank careened around the corner he had a terrible surprise. He slammed into Arnold Stockard! The CompuCar owner had trudged up the seven flights of stairs in search of Hartman and the Hardys. Unfortunately, he found them at just the wrong time!

Stockard was a big, heavy man. Frank was no lightweight, but he was no match for Stockard's massive girth. Even though he was racing down the stairs, Frank didn't fall forward. He bounced off Stockard and fell back into Joe.

Joe tried to get out of the way, but he couldn't.

The two brothers collided and Joe fell backward, his hands instinctively flying back out to break his fall. The box containing the master computer disks soared out of Joe's hands. They sailed in the direction of his fall, landing halfway back up the stairwell.

Before Frank or Joe could recuperate from their falls, Hartman moved nimbly down the stairs, kneeled, and picked up the box holding the master computer disks.

"It would seem," said Hartman, smirking, "that your gamble didn't pay off. In fact, things have worked out even better than I had hoped. I'll now have the honor of destroying the CompuCar Company in the presence of the man I most thoroughly detest."

"Me?" asked Stockard, picking himself up off the stairwell landing.

"An excellent deduction," Hartman said with grim satisfaction. "I'll get special pleasure out of watching you see your company fall into total, irreversible ruin."

"What do you want?" pleaded Stockard. "I'll pay you. Just don't ruin the company or hurt anyone else. What's your price?"

"Sorry, I don't have time to negotiate with you," said Hartman in a voice tinged with madness. "The police are coming. They're going to catch me. Too bad it won't do you or your company any good. By the time they find us in my lab, the CompuCar Company will be history!"

Joe looked longingly at the small box in Hartman's hands. He couldn't believe he had lost it. Somehow, they had to get those disks back.

"Get moving," ordered Hartman. He pointed his pistol at them. "And I'll shoot any one of you who makes a move in the wrong direction."

Stockard went first, followed by Frank and Joe. Edward Hartman trailed behind them, his gun aimed at their backs.

When they reached the lab, Frank got a brief glimpse out the window and saw a police car in the parking lot below. The police had arrived, but it looked like they'd

137

never get up there in time to stop Hartman. If anyone was going to stop it, it was going to have to be Frank and Joe.

The lab itself was a small room on the eighth floor. It had a desk with a computer on it, and a long table loaded with glass beakers, test tubes, and bottles holding all sorts of multicolored liquids. They sat atop burners that were turned off.

No one spoke as they all squeezed into the lab. In the background they could hear the constant clanging of the elevator doors out in the hallway. It was like a mechanical heartbeat gone wild as the banging doors opened and closed in a rhythm all their own. The heartbeats of Frank and Joe, however, were pounding even faster.

"Move over in front of the desk," commanded Hartman. "I want to be able to see all three of you while I'm typing new directions onto the master disks. And when I'm through, I'm going to slip them into the main computer . . . and then it's goodbye, CompuCar." He chuckled. "I've waited a long time for this moment. Who said revenge isn't sweet?"

He turned on a desk lamp that was connected to a small power generator on the floor. It was the same power source for his computer. Frank thought that it had been clever of Hartman to separate himself from the factory's virus-infested machinery.

Hartman opened the box holding the master disks and put one of them into his desktop computer. He began tapping away at the keys with one hand while holding the gun on Stockard and the Hardys with the other.

Hartman was careful. His eyes kept flitting back and forth between the keyboard and his three prisoners. It might have slowed his programming, but his constant checking stopped Frank and Joe from trying anything desperate.

"Done with the first disk," Hartman cheerfully announced. "Just two more to go."

He took the second disk out of the box, inserted it in the computer, and began to type.

Arnold Stockard looked like a beaten man. His face sagged, his arms hung limp at his sides. He felt helpless to stop his employee's vengeful destruction. Everything he had built was crumbling around him. And now he was suffering the final humiliation. The master CompuCar disks that were the foundation of his company were being destroyed.

Stockard, however, didn't realize what Frank and Joe already knew—that the virus in these master disks would spread to computers everywhere. Stockard's problems would be minor compared to the chaos caused by this virus spreading throughout the world's computers. That's why Frank and Joe couldn't afford to give up the way Stockard had. They had to act.

While Hartman typed away at the second disk, the Hardy brothers each tried to figure out what they could do to stop him.

Then, Frank spotted the electric cord coming out of Hartman's computer. It hung down the side of the desk where it was plugged into the softly humming generator. He considered trying to dislodge the cord with a kick and turn off the machine. But the more he thought about it, the less he liked the idea. At best, he'd turn the computer off for a minute. And during that minute, Edward Hartman would kill all three of them.

Meanwhile, Joe realized that they could use the desk right in front of them to stop Hartman. If they could lift it and send it crashing over at the computer genius before he could react and shoot, they'd have him nailed. Joe scanned the desk, judging its weight. It was a heavy, steel desk, but if he could get Frank and Stockard to make their move at the same time, they just might be able to dump it over on top of Hartman.

Except there was one other problem.

Out of the corner of his eye, Joe saw a bolt holding one of the desk's legs to the floor. He looked at the other legs. They were all secured to the floor so that the desk wouldn't move.

Hartman laughed to himself, then he raised his eyes from the computer screen. "That's the second disk. Just one more to go. Are you enjoying this, Stockard?" he said, gloating.

Stockard didn't answer. He turned his head away.

As the computer virus was being typed into the third and last disk, Frank and Joe racked their brains for something—anything—they could do that would have even the slightest chance of working.

Frank wished that those elevator doors would stop banging. The noise was unnerving him. It reminded him of what was going to happen throughout the world when computer-controlled machines started coming down with Hartman's virus.

And then it hit him. The sound of the elevator doors had given him an idea. If the computer-controlled elevators had gone nuts, then anything else that was operated by the building's computer would also go crazy when it was turned on.

The question was, what would really happen if he flicked on the air conditioning? What if he turned on the overhead lights? The results, he hoped, would be similar to what had happened in their CC-2000. In other words, *anything* might happen. For all he knew, turning on the overhead lights might cause the phones to ring. That was hardly going to help them.

He couldn't possibly guess the results once his plan was put into motion. He'd be gambling with their lives, but there was no other choice. But first, he had to somehow let Joe in on his idea without alerting Hartman.

"You were pretty smart to put that generator in here," Frank began, hoping that Joe would eventually catch on to what he was trying to say.

Hartman banged his fist on the desk top. "You made me type in the wrong command," he snarled. "Stop trying to distract me."

"I'm not trying to distract you," Frank quickly countered. "I was just impressed with how you set yourself up here so that you wouldn't have to use things like the air conditioning, the lights, and everything else you infected with this virus. Like our car."

Hartman stopped typing and looked up with a scowl on his face. "I told you to shut up!" he shouted. "If you don't, I'll shut you up—permanently. Understand?"

"I understand," said Frank. "Sorry."

When Hartman turned his attention back to the complicated command he was typing onto the disk, Frank glanced at his brother.

Joe smiled and gave a subtle nod of his head.

He had gotten the message.

"There!" crowed Hartman, pulling the third disk out of his computer. "That's all finished. And Mr. Arnold Stockard," he added scornfully, "you're almost finished, too. When these disks are inserted into the main factory computer, my revenge will be complete."

"You're a sick man," Stockard mumbled.

"Sick?" cried the enraged scientist. "Wronged, is more like it!" he accused.

Stockard shook his head sadly. "You had no head for business," he said softly. "You'd never have built this company the way I did. I took your ideas and made them work. Besides, I gave you credit for all your scientific achievements and I paid you well from the very beginning."

"No!" shouted Hartman. "I could have done it myself. This should have been my company, not yours!"

Without realizing it, Stockard had created just the diversion Frank and Joe needed. As Hartman ranted and raved, the Hardys gradually eased backward toward the wall.

The switches for the air conditioning and the overhead lights were just a few yards away. If they could only get a little bit closer.

Suddenly, Hartman sensed that Frank and Joe had moved away. Realizing that they were up to something, he demanded, "Where do you think you're going?" He swung his pistol in their direction.

"Now!" shouted Frank.

16 Saved by a Glitch

Frank hit the overhead light switch. Instead of the lights, however, the sprinkler system turned on, sending a spray of water raining down on them!

The sudden shower made it difficult to see in the already dimly lit room. It was even harder for Hartman to see because his glasses had instantly fogged up. If his vision hadn't been clouded, he might have seen the result of Joe's hitting of the air-conditioning switch.

It didn't get colder in the lab, it got hotter—and in some very specific places. While they were being soaked by the sprinkler system, the burners underneath all the beakers and test tubes had suddenly been switched on. The mysterious liquids quickly began to bubble and boil. But Frank and Joe ignored the flames. They had more immediate problems.

Hartman turned wildly at each new noise, aiming his gun wildly. "You won't get away!" he screamed.

But Frank and Joe didn't want to escape. Not yet anyway. First they wanted those master computer disks.

But they also had to get Arnold Stockard out of Hartman's way. The CompuCar owner was standing still, befuddled by everything that was happening around him. Hartman might start firing at any moment, and Stockard made an awfully big target.

Joe dove at Stockard's legs and tackled him, bringing him crashing to the floor and out of the way of Hartman's gun.

Frank went after the computer disks. Crawling along the wet, slippery floor, he made his way around Hartman's desk.

Suddenly smoke began pouring out of several of the overheated beakers and tubes.

Hartman finally saw the blue flames burning underneath the sensitive chemical solutions. He circled away from Frank in a mad rush, hoping to turn them off. Except the switches under the burners didn't work— they turned on the overhead lights!

While Hartman was busy with the burners, Frank stood up. He saw the three master disks on top of the desk and grabbed them.

He was about to yell out to Joe and Arnold

Stockard that they should make a run for it, when he suddenly heard a loud hissing noise coming from the boiling beakers.

"They're going to blow!" cried Hartman with a look of terror on his face. "I can't turn off the burners!"

Frank didn't waste any time. He dropped the disks back on the desk, jumped up on the table, and then dove through the air at Hartman. He landed on the scientist's back and wrestled him to the floor.

They both landed with a heavy thud, Frank lying on top of the frightened and startled Hartman. A second later, the boiling liquids did just what the scientist said they would do.

They blew up.

The explosion was deafening. The room filled with yellowish smoke as white-hot glass shards cut through the lab like a million needles. If Frank hadn't knocked Hartman down, both he and the scientist would have been ripped to shreds.

Meanwhile, Joe kept Stockard down on the ground, covering him with his body. And Frank stayed on top of Hartman for two reasons: to protect him from harm, and to make sure he didn't get away!

They had been lucky. The gas cloud would have killed them if the explosion hadn't blown out the only window in the lab. The open window had let the fresh air inside.

The walls of the lab looked like pin cushions. Little slivers of hot, melting glass were stuck everywhere—in the ceiling, in the door, in the walls. But happily not in Frank, Joe, Stockard, or Hartman.

"What's going on here?" demanded a familiar voice. Frank and Joe looked up and saw Chief Collig, huffing and puffing from his eight-story run up the stairwell. He stood in the doorway with his gun drawn, staring at the incredible scene in the lab.

Con Riley was right behind him. "Looks like a tornado hit this room," he said.

"Where have you been?" Joe asked with a crooked smile on his face as he helped Arnold Stockard to his feet.

"We got here as fast as we could," said Riley, "but after we arrived, we didn't know where to find you. And there's a problem with the elevators."

"Though we had a pretty good idea where you were when we heard the first explosions," added Collig. "We just didn't know if there'd be anything left of you when we got here.

"Now," he continued, "would somebody please tell me what this is all about?"

Frank stood, helping Hartman to his feet. "Here's your saboteur," he announced.

A sour look creased Chief Collig's face. "Are you sure?" he asked.

Joe bristled. "We nearly got shot, blown up, torn apart, and gassed because of this guy," he said, pointing at Hartman. "He didn't do all that because we caught him jaywalking."

Frank chuckled.

"What are *you* laughing at?" asked Joe, turning to his brother.

"You. I seem to remember you saying something about becoming more tactful. Remember?"

"Give me a break, huh?" Joe said with a groan.

"We'd better put the cuffs on him," suggested Riley, who started to walk past the chief.

"Just a minute," said Collig, blocking Riley with his arm. He turned to Frank and Joe. "Do you have any proof that this man is the saboteur?"

Suddenly Arnold Stockard's voice boomed in the glass-strewn lab. "I am Arnold Stockard, owner and president of the CompuCar Company. The Hardys and I are three witnesses to a complete confession that Edward Hartman committed the sabotage," he stated. "Frank and Joe Hardy saved my company and my life. And that's a fact."

"Well, that's good enough . . . I guess," said Collig. "Put on the cuffs."

Stockard watched as Detective Riley handcuffed Hartman's hands together. The scientist didn't seem to know what was happening. With his revenge no longer possible, he lost the little bit of sanity he had left.

"Just a minute," said the president of the CompuCar Company as Riley led Hartman toward the door. "An awful lot of people think I'm just a businessman without any scruples," he said softly. "Let them think what they want, but I know that Edward isn't a criminal. He's ill, sick; he didn't know what he was doing. I don't want him to go to prison. I want him to get help. Please see to it, Chief, and I'll pay all the medical costs. Every penny."

"You don't have to do that," said Collig. "You aren't responsible for his actions."

"Yes, I am," whispered Stockard. "I wanted this company to be a success so badly that I drove him to it. I *am* responsible."

Joe was impressed. "I didn't think very much of you throughout this case," he said.

150

"I'm glad I was wrong. I'm proud that Frank and I were able to work for you."

Arnold Stockard rubbed his eyes with his left hand and said, "I owe the two of you an awful lot. You not only saved my company, you saved my life—in more ways than one. I don't know how to thank you."

Frank smiled. "Just let us borrow another CC-2000 sometime," he said, grinning. "One *without* a virus."

When Frank and Joe arrived home later that night, they were happy to find that their father was back from his case up in Boston.

"How did it go?" Frank asked.

"Just fine," he reported. "I caught the thieves in the sting operation I set up and we recovered all the stolen property. It went without a hitch. What about you?" he asked. "Mom was telling me that you just started on a case."

"Nope," said Joe, with a straight face. "That's all over."

Their father looked disturbed. "What happened? Did you lose the client?" he asked.

Joe grinned. "No. We solved the case."

"In just two days?"

"Hey," said Frank, joining in on the fun

with Joe, "we're Fenton Hardy's sons. Solving cases comes naturally."

Their father laughed. He was very proud of his sons.

Then the elder Mr. Hardy eased back in his chair and changed the subject, saying, "Your mother was also telling me that you've been having trouble with your van."

"We checked the engine, the electrical system, everything," complained Frank. "We can't figure it out. The thing just won't run. Would you take a look at it for us?"

"Already did," announced their father. Then a broad smile lit up his face. "I'm glad you're better detectives than you are mechanics," he said. "You were out of gas."